# Cowboy's Conundrum

Culpepper Cowboys Book 3

Kirsten Osbourne

Joy Quinlan has spent her entire life trying to be the personification of her name. When she moves to Wyoming with her three sisters, she is determined to keep looking happy, as she always has. She worries that none of the four exciting Culpepper men will be interested in her, but sexy Kolby makes a beeline for her as soon as they meet.

Kolby Culpepper has known for years that his heart must remain removed from any relationship. When he spots Joy sitting on his mother's sofa, he knows she's the Quinlan Quad for him, but he becomes more determined than ever to keep from loving again. Will this unlikely pair be able to see past their hang-ups? Or are they destined to spend the rest of their lives without love?

# Chapter 1

Joy kept smiling as they drove the last few miles to the Culpepper Ranch. She knew that's what her sisters needed from her, so that's what she gave them. All six girls in her family had silly names, but only she was expected to live up to hers. Since she was a tiny girl, she'd known it was her role in life to be joyful, and so she'd been joyful.

The others were really on her nerves—especially Hope and Chastity. Chastity was a pain in her backside, as usual, but it was Hope's reaction that really annoyed Joy. She knew Chastity was a brat, but Hope knew she was too. Usually Hope didn't let Chastity bother her the way she was then. Of course, with this being their third day in the car, they were all feeling angrier than usual. The long trip had been a test of their loyalty to one another. As quadruplets, they'd always functioned as a unit, and they still were. Right then, they were just a very angry unit.

When they stopped in front of the huge one-story ranch house, Joy opened her car door and walked away from the car—away from the house. She needed a minute before she met or talked to anyone, or she wouldn't be able to fulfill her role in this world. Taking deep breaths, she stared off at the mountains in the distance, realizing those mountains might just be her center here in Wyoming.

She could hear excitement behind her, but she had no desire to join in. She was going to meet her future husband in a few minutes, and she really needed to be able to live up to expectations when she did.

Finally, she felt like she could smile, and be the joyous woman she was expected to be, so she turned and walked toward the house. Her sisters who were with her, Hope, Faith, and Chastity, had already gone into the house with Dr. Lachele and Linda Culpepper, her future mother-in-law. As long as one of the men was interested in her, at least. She worried the men would all want her sisters and none would be willing to even look at her.

Joy felt like she was too awkward to ever really find a man who would care about her. She'd never been kissed, but as far as she knew, out of the four of them only Chastity had been. Chastity made it her business in life not to live up to her name.

Opening the front door, Joy walked into the house, smiling sweetly. Dr. Lachele rushed over to her, hugging her tightly. "Joy! It's good to see you!"

Joy had a special fondness for Dr. Lachele, but really, she couldn't think of anyone who wouldn't. The woman just lit up a room as soon as she entered it. Between her purple hair and colorful language, she was truly special. "I'm glad to finally be here!"

Dr. Lachele looked at Joy, studying her for a moment. "Rough car trip?"

Joy smiled, feeling like her face would break. "It was long." For once, she would like to yell and scream about how awful her sisters had acted, but she wouldn't.

"I'm sure it was. I know you four are close, being quadruplets raised as you were, you'd have to be. But two-and-a-half days in a car with three siblings? I don't care if you're in your seventies. Someone is going to want to kill someone else!"

"Are you putting on your psychologist hat with me, Dr. Lachele?"

"Do I need to?" Dr. Lachele, took Joy's arm, pulling her a bit down the hallway and lowering her voice. "I worry about you. Your sisters are so easy to read, but you—you always have the exact same smile on your face. It's like you are incapable of showing any emotion that isn't positive."

Joy shrugged. "I'm Joy."

"You don't always have to exemplify your name, you know."

"I'll keep that in mind," Joy said, with the exact same smile on her face Dr. Lachele had just complained about.

Dr. Lachele sighed, obviously concerned. "You have my number. Please make sure you use it if you need me."

"I do. I'm sure you'll be visiting to check on us as well."

"Of course I will. Don't do anything you don't want to do, Joy. Live for yourself for a change."

"I'll do my best." But Joy knew she wouldn't. It was her job to make the people around her happy. Her mother had told her that repeatedly over the years.

Joy moved around Dr. Lachele to where Chastity was leaned over a countertop talking to a blond woman. She looked to be in her early fifties, so Joy assumed she was their future mother-in-law.

The woman looked up and smiled. "You must be Joy!"

Joy nodded, feeling ridiculously shy. "Yes, ma'am. Are you Mrs. Culpepper?"

The woman laughed. "Well, only if you're feeling very formal. Call me Linda!"

Joy smiled and nodded. "Sounds good. Thank you for letting us stay with you for a while. Your home is lovely." She looked around her, spotting Faith sitting off by herself on the sofa. There was no sign of Hope. She must have needed a minute to herself as well. Not sure what to do with herself, she wandered over to sit beside Faith. "She seems nice," she said in a whisper.

Faith nodded. "She really does. Are you as happy to be out of that car as I am?"

"I really thought Hope was going to strangle Chastity for a minute there, and I wouldn't have blamed her!" Joy shook her head. "So happy to finally be here."

"Are you calling Mom and Dad tonight?"

Joy frowned. "I don't want to, but one of us has to. I don't plan on telling them where we are, just that we've found some nice Christian men and are being well-chaperoned." Difficult talks with their parents always fell to Joy. She wasn't certain why, but it had always been that way.

"Good idea." Faith looked over the top of Joy's head at something. "Oh, my! I call dibs on the sexy one!"

Joy turned her head, wishing immediately she had a tissue. "Am I drooling?" she asked softly. "All three of them are sexy!" She'd been attracted to a few boys in college, and she'd once even had a crush, but these three weren't boys. They were men with a capital M.

"Which one do you like?" Faith asked, her voice a whisper.

"The one in the middle." Joy had always been fond of dark men, and that Culpepper Cowboy had hair as black as night. She wanted that one, but really? They were all pretty darned sexy, making her feel things in the pit of her stomach. Would she really be married to one of them within a month? Sleeping with him?

Faith sighed. "I don't know how we're ever going to choose!"

* * *

"Let me help!" Chris said, his voice filled with exasperation.

Karlan handed him a board. "Sure, hold this." He went back to work on the fence, pounding in a nail and wrapping barbed wire around it. "By this time next year, I think we'll be able to afford electric fences."

Kolby glanced over his shoulder. "Those cost an arm and a leg. How could we do that with the kind of acreage we're looking at fencing in?"

Karlan shrugged. "A little at a time, I guess."

Kolby looked down at his watch for the third time in five minutes. "Aren't any of you guys as nervous as I am?"

"Nervous?" Karlan asked, his voice perfectly calm. "What's there to be nervous about?"

Kolby shook his head, refusing to believe none of his three brothers had profusely sweating palms like he did. Within a few hours they were all going to meet four women, and they were required to choose one to marry, and marry her, within a month. How could they do that? He took a deep breath. "What if they're all money-hungry snobs, who've come here thinking ranch life is like they've seen on *Dallas*?"

"Don't be a nervous twit, Kolby. Dr. Lachele vetted them. My friend Trey says she's brilliant at what she does," Chris said, still holding the board. "What do you want me to do with this, Karlan?"

Karlan shook his head at his brother. "Just keep holding it!"

Kolby frowned. "I'm not being a nervous twit. Did your friend Trey tell you about how crazy Dr. Lachele was? Did he mention her purple hair and strange outlook on life?"

Chris shook his head. "Well, no, but she wouldn't send women we shouldn't marry."

Karlan's text tone sounded, and he reached into his pocket for his phone. "They're here. Mom says to get to the big house right away."

Chris looked at the board he was holding. "What should I do with this?"

"Oh, just lean it up against the fence post. You can hold it again next time," Karlan responded.

Chris rolled his eyes but did as he was told.

Kolby took a deep breath, trying to calm his nervous stomach. How was he supposed to find someone to spend the rest of his life with? Was divorce a possibility? He needed to reread the contract as soon as he could.

He mounted his horse, following his brothers. What if there wasn't one he liked? Or worse—what if there was? Would he be able to hide his emotions? He couldn't give a woman the kind of power over him that Rachelle had wielded. He'd carried an engagement ring around in his pocket, looking for just the right moment. Then she'd gone to volunteer at the underwear model shoot. After the snow had cleared, Rachelle had admitted she'd spent the four days of the blizzard doing the horizontal polka with one of the models. He still had the ring.

He forced all thoughts of Rachelle from his mind. Rachelle was the past, and he was about to meet his future. Whatever her name was.

When they reached the house, Karlan veered toward the back. "You go on!" he called.

Kolby, Cooper, and Chris went to the front door and into the house. Kolby's eyes immediately caught a girl with bright red hair and green eyes, who was sitting on the couch with a girl who must have been her sister. He was too intent on the red head to notice a resemblance. Oh the girl made his heart beat faster!

He walked to the couch and stopped a foot behind it, her eyes wide as she stared up at him. "Hi. I'm Kolby."

"Hi, Kolby," said the girl, her voice soft and sweet. "I'm Joy."

"You certainly bring me joy."

Joy's face lit up with a smile. He was a romantic. That's what she needed. A man who would bring romance to her life. Her sisters didn't need the kind of romance she did. Faith just wanted to work on her babies. Hope wanted to control the world. Chastity only needed sex, and a lot of it. But Joy needed love and romance.

She was aware of Faith talking to one of his brothers, and Chastity falling all over herself for another. She blocked them all out though. Kolby. Kolby was meant for her, and she was going to take advantage of that fact. "Tell me about yourself."

Kolby walked around the long couch and sat on the loveseat that was at a ninety-degree angle to it. He patted the spot beside him, and Joy stood up, moving to sit where he'd indicated. "Hi," she said again.

Kolby grinned at her, his arm going to the back of the couch, not exactly around her, but it felt like it. "Hi," his voice was deep and a bit gruff. Just hearing him speak sent a little thrill through her body. "I'm a cowboy. We three older brothers work the ranch, while Chris, the youngest is an itinerate science teacher."

Joy nodded. She could understand him wanting to go his own way. "I see. Do you like being a cowboy?"

He smiled. "There's nothing else in this world I'd rather be doing. I love to be out on the range, the sun and wind on my skin. I love being on horseback as we move the herd. I'm not big on mending fences, but I'll do it when I need to."

"Sounds like you're living the life you want to live." She liked that idea. Being married to a man who was happy with what he did, would make it easier on her.

"I am. I guess I never realized just how privileged I am. I may not be a rich man, but a man is always blessed if he can wake up in the morning and do what he wants to do more than anything."

Joy nodded, her face lit up. "That's right. It must be an amazing feeling to do just what you want to do."

"You don't do what you want to do? What was your job back home? I don't even know where you're from!"

Joy made a face. "I'm from a small town in Kentucky, and I've never had a job. Our parents thought that our jobs should be looking for husbands and learning to be good wives. I've never even had a job as simple as flipping burgers."

"Well, I don't know that you should have had a job flipping burgers," Kolby said with a wink, "but something would be good! What do you do with all your time?"

"We all have crafts we enjoy. Hope sews and spends a lot of time volunteering with children. Faith makes the most beautiful dolls you've ever seen. Chastity knits, and she makes wonderful socks."

Kolby couldn't help but notice she left out what she did. "And Joy? What does Joy do?"

Joy frowned. "Do you promise not to laugh?"

He nodded solemnly. "Why would I laugh?"

"I make houses and furniture for Barbie dolls out of plastic canvas." Her words were merely a mumble, like she was ashamed of her craft.

"Really? I've never even heard of such a thing. What's plastic canvas?"

Joy jumped up from the loveseat and went to fetch the small bag that was leaning up against the couch where his brother, Cooper, now sat with one of her sisters. She sat back down beside him, a little closer this time. She wanted to feel his warmth. Reaching into her bag, she pulled out a small rectangle of plastic canvas. "This is what it looks like before it's worked." Then she held up the bag itself, which was three different shades of green in a pattern. "This is what it looks like worked. This bag was one of my first projects."

"And you make stuff for Barbies from it?" He knew what a Barbie doll was, of course, because everyone did, but he'd never really been up close and personal with one. They'd lived out in the country his whole life, and he only had brothers. His only cousin was male. How would he have been around Barbies?

"Yes." Joy's eyes were dancing as she stuck her hand back into her bag again, this time pulling out a book. "These are instructions on how to make a castle."

"A castle? You can make a castle from that stuff?"

"I love doing it! It's fun for me. My sisters and I will all sit around and talk while we work on our crafts. Well, all except for Grace, but she talks to us while her cakes are baking."

"Okay, so how many sisters are there total? Just the four of you who came?"

Joy shook her head. "No there are six total. Four came here..." She trailed off, leaving the words "to marry you and your brothers," unspoken. "Hope, Faith, Chastity and I are quadruplets. Grace and Honor are our little sisters. They're two years younger than us."

"Twins? No boys?"

"Nope. Just the six of us."

Kolby wiped the back of his hand across his brow. "That's a lot of girls to look out for."

Joy shrugged. "Our parents were so strict it didn't seem to matter. We were only allowed out of their sight when absolutely necessary. We were never allowed extracurricular activities. I think that was mainly due to Chastity, though."

"Chastity?" he asked. "Which one is Chastity?"

Joy realized then that this man really didn't know her sisters. She'd never had to introduce her sisters to anyone, because they were something of a legend in their home town. Quadruplets weren't the norm anywhere. "There," she said, pointing toward the kitchen where Chastity stood with one of his brothers. Chastity was rubbing on his brother's arm and making eyes in a way that made Joy deeply embarrassed for her sister. Instead of continuing to watch, she pointed out the others. "That's Faith." She pointed to the other couch where Faith sat with another of his brothers. "I think Hope is still on the back porch, but I'm not sure."

Kolby nodded. "Back porch, huh? That explains where Karlan went."

"I'm sorry?" Joy had no idea what he was talking about.

"When we got to the house, Karlan went to the back porch, and Cooper, Chris, and I went to the front door. Karlan must be with your sister, Hope." He shook his head. "Did your parents stop having kids because they ran out of names?"

Joy shook her head. "Oh, no. They had Charity, Patience, Prudence, and Harmony all ready, in case they had another set of quadruplets."

"Do any of your sisters suit their names?" he asked, a half-grin on his face.

She shook her head. "Not a one of them. Grace is the clumsiest girl you ever did see. Chastity, well, we're not going to talk about Chastity. She's technically chaste, even if her thoughts are far from it! Hope is usually hopeful, but she has her moments of doubt. Honor has honor, I guess. As much as anyone, but not more so. Faith has faith, but again, about like anyone."

"And Joy? Is she filled with Joy?" Kolby couldn't believe the odd conversation he was having with her. He reached out and traced her cheek with his index finger.

Joy nodded. "My parents always talked about how I was the only one to really live up to my name." She didn't mention what a turmoil her thoughts usually were. She wasn't trying to deceive him, but what man would want a woman who wasn't joyous?

He smiled at that. "I like that quality in a woman." He wanted to kiss her. He'd met her fifteen minutes before, and already all he could think about was kissing her. She'd be fine to have babies with, but he really didn't want to lose his heart.

They both jumped when the back door opened and Hope came in with his brother. Karlan, she thought. He announced they were getting married. Joy's eyes widened. Already? She'd expected Hope to be the first among them to marry, but to be engaged within fifteen minutes? Hope did everything first, but this was extreme even for her.

Joy stood and walked to where Karlan and Hope were talking, sensing that Kolby was right behind her.

After a brief discussion they left again, and Joy looked at Kolby with surprise. "Well, that was quick."

Kolby rolled his eyes. "Just like Karlan. He found the one he wanted and immediately proposed so there was no chance of anyone else getting her."

Joy bit her lip. "Does that mean you'd rather be with Hope as well?"

He opened his mouth to reassure her but thought better of it. "I don't know. I've never met the girl. I've only met you."

Joy nodded slowly. Of all the sisters, she was the only one who wasn't asked out on a regular basis. She had always felt miniscule when compared to the personalities of her sisters. "Would you like me to introduce you to the others?"

He shook his head. "Not now. Let's go for a quick walk."

"A walk?" Joy was confused. Didn't he care when Hope and Karlan were getting married? Surely he did.

He nodded firmly. "A walk. I want to get to know you without all these eyes on us."

Joy looked around the room. She didn't feel any eyes on her. Linda and Dr. Lachele were talking. Hope was on the back porch with Karlan. Faith was still on the couch with one of his brothers, and Chastity was—well, it looked like Chastity was trying to lose her virginity in the dining room, but that was neither here nor there.

"Okay," she said, not certain what bug had crawled up his butt, but she didn't really care to find out. She was tugged toward the front door by him, smiling tightly at Faith as she passed her on her way out.

When they reached the open air, he kept her hand in his, walking around the side of the house toward the stable. "I don't know what you know about the ranch yet. We have five houses here, one for each of us, and Mom lives here in the big house."

"I see." What she saw were mountains off in the distance, and she wanted to go to them. She wanted to drag Kolby off and beg him to have a picnic at the base of one of the mountains. She wanted romance in her world. She wasn't so certain that Kolby would be able to deliver on that as she had been in the moments after they'd first met.

"I've lived here since my dad died when I was two."

"I'm sorry. You must not have any memories of him."

He shook his head. "No, I don't. My granddaddy made a great substitute father, but I always felt like something was missing."

"I can understand that."

Kolby walked down a path of rocks with animals painted on them toward a small bench. Once he reached the bench, he sat down, turning to face Joy. "I didn't really want to walk."

Joy stared at him with wide eyes. "What did you want?"

"I wanted to kiss you somewhere we wouldn't be seen."

"K...k...kiss me?" She'd never been kissed in her life. She'd have been astonished to hear anyone had ever wanted to kiss her.

He nodded. "Do you mind?"

Joy swallowed hard. "I guess not. No one has ever kissed me before." As soon as she'd blurted the words out, she was embarrassed by them. She shouldn't have told him that. What would he think of her?

He stared at her in shock. "You've never had a boyfriend?"

Joy shook her head. "No, we were never allowed to. Our parents firmly believed that your first kiss should take place after you speak your vows before a pastor."

"Wow." Kolby wasn't even sure what to say to that. "I didn't know there were any girls who were even virgins in this country past the age of twenty, let alone un-kissed." He frowned at her. "Please tell me you're over twenty?" His voice was slightly panicked.

She giggled at that. "We're twenty-two."

"Oh, good. I won't feel so much like I'm cradle-robbing then." He was twenty-nine, which was seven years older than her, but that didn't bother him like her being under twenty would have. He stroked her cheek with one hand, moving his fingers into her hair, and tilting her head to one side. "I'm going to kiss you, Miss Joy."

Joy nodded, her eyes drifting closed as his mouth came down on hers. His lips were soft, gently moving against her closed mouth. She put her hand on his shoulder, unsure what she was supposed to do to participate in the kiss. Her parents had never kissed in front of them, and she'd never been allowed to watch much television. Kisses were foreign to her.

He raised his head, a grin on his lips. "Yup. You definitely live up to your name. That kiss brought me joy."

She smiled at him, blushing slightly. She liked that kiss. It was nice. Chastity had talked to her about kisses with tongues, but she knew it would be a long time before she was ready for something like that. Years maybe!

"I'm glad," she whispered. "I think I like kissing."

He chuckled, already feeling the tug of his heart. This girl was awfully special. "We should probably go back in and see when Karlan and Hope are going to marry. I have a feeling we'll be attending a wedding today."

"Do you really think they'll do it that quickly?"

"If I know my brother, and I do, he's already called the preacher."

# Chapter 2

During the short reception Linda had for Karlan and Hope, which took place just hours after they'd met, the men's cousin showed up. He made some demands and threatened to take them to court before leaving. In short, he wanted one fifth of the ranch, and nothing else would satisfy him.

After he'd gone, the sisters all exchanged glances, and Joy could see there was already a plan. Whatever it was, she was on board, of course. She had marketable skills and would happily use them.

After they'd all had a light snack, Kolby once again asked Joy to go for a walk. She agreed, explaining to Linda where she was going. She could tell it annoyed Kolby a little, but she knew that Linda was acting as her chaperone, and she wasn't about to be rude to her.

He led her a different way this time, explaining the layout of the ranch. "I really want to show you my house."

Joy glanced up at him in the late afternoon sunlight. "You know I'm not willing to...get frisky with you, don't you?"

He laughed, the sound filling her with delight. "Yes, I know. No hanky-panky or premarital diddling. I've been given the same memo you have." Dr. Lachele had made all of them sign contracts explaining about no pre-marital sex, and all of the sisters had to be married within a month of their arrival or the men had to settle ten-thousand dollars on any who weren't.

She blushed. "Well, that's fine then."

"I just want you to see my house. I want you to know where you're going to live if we end up tying the knot."

"All right." She followed him to a small house and waited as he opened the door for her. She noted that he didn't bother with a key. She'd lived in a small town, but they'd still felt the need to lock their doors. She liked the idea of living somewhere where people didn't bother with locks.

Walking into the house, she immediately noted that it was bigger than she'd thought. As she stepped inside, there was a kitchen and connected dining room off to the left. To her right was a living room, complete with a large screen television. She wondered if he watched television in the evenings, and her mind's eye saw the two of them sitting cozily on his couch, her working on her plastic canvas and him watching the TV. It sounded lovely to her.

His room was big, with a bed definitely large enough for two. There was a connecting bath with both tub and separate shower. Then they walked down the hall in the other direction and there were two rooms that seemed to be used for storage more than anything else.

As she peered into one of the rooms, she smiled, noting the windows were facing the east. "I'd love to use this room as a craft room."

Kolby nodded. "I think that would be fine." He caught her hand, pulling her toward the living room and the comfortable-looking couch. Sitting down, he drew her down beside him. "Now, I want to introduce you to something most girls learn when they're teenagers."

Her eyes focused on the television. Would he show her some sit-coms? She'd always wanted to sit for hours in front of the TV with her crafts. "What's that?"

"Making out!"

She laughed. "I don't know if your mother would exactly approve of that."

He looked over his shoulder. "I don't think she's here!"

"Well, no, but I think while she's my chaperone, we should at least be cognizant of what she'd approve of."

He sighed. "I just want to kiss you. If I promise to keep my hands above the shoulders, would that help?"

Joy thought about it for a moment before nodding. "I think that would be fine then."

As he was lowering his head toward hers, he whispered, "You can put your hands anywhere you want, baby!"

His lips descended on hers as she stifled her laugh, her hands automatically going to the back of his neck. When his tongue came out to touch her lip, she was startled at first, but then she realized she liked it. She moved closer to him, and he moved his hand to her back.

She pulled away to look up at him. "That's below the neck."

"It's your back! Even Dr. Lachele would say that's perfectly fine." He kissed her again, this time his tongue found the seam of her lips, tempting her to open for him.

Joy opened her mouth tentatively, wondering at what he would do. She felt like a child, not knowing anything about kissing, but at least she was willing to learn. When his tongue entered her mouth and stroked hers, she let out a gasp of surprise. She'd thought Chastity was making things up when she talked about how she'd kissed Bobby Banks at church one Sunday morning.

She felt the kiss all the way through her, her body coming alive for him. Wanting to be closer, she imagined being in his arms with nothing between them. She pulled away, knowing why her parents had wanted them to wait for their first kiss.

Kolby took deep, gulping breaths. "I need to get you back to my mom's house."

Joy nodded. "I think that would be wise. I like kissing you a little bit more than I should, Kolby Culpepper."

"I'm very glad to hear that, Joy." He wanted a passionate woman in his arms, even if he was worried he might fall in love with her. Getting to his feet, he caught her hand and pulled her to hers. "Don't get too comfortable at Mom's house."

She looked at the back of his head as he pulled her toward the door, and she wondered briefly if he would always feel the need to pull her around like a child's toy. Joy was so glad he'd chosen her. She'd fully expected to be the last of the four sisters to be chosen by one of the men.

As they walked back to his mother's house in the dark of the spring evening, she rested her head against his shoulder. Being accepted by him was important to her, and she was so thankful, he'd not turned his nose up at her craft. Why, even her sisters made fun of it at times.

At the front door, he pulled her into his arms and kissed her again. "One to sleep on," he whispered.

Joy smiled up at him, thankful he was there beside her. "Will we spend tomorrow together?" she asked.

He shook his head. "I'll be here for lunch, but my brothers and I will be working most of the day. We need to talk to figure out a plan for buying Travis out."

Joy squeezed his hand. "Don't worry too much about the money. We'll help."

Kolby nodded, pretending to understand her. Four women who had little training and had never worked, trying to help, didn't seem like such a wonderful thing to him. Hopefully they had hidden talents somewhere. He didn't want to have to send his new wife off to wait tables in town, but he sure would if it was the only way to keep the ranch.

Joy stopped in the kitchen to get a drink of water, noticing that Dr. Lachele and Linda were still talking non-stop. "Have you two been friends long?" she asked.

Linda laughed. "I met her when she came to do her testing on my sons. We just hit it off."

Joy smiled. "I love friendships like that." She'd had one or two, but her parents had always stopped them quickly. They'd thought having five sisters should always be enough, and there was no need for any of them to seek friendship outside the family.

"Did you have a nice time with Kolby?" Linda asked, her eyes seeming to know exactly what Joy and Kolby had been doing.

Joy nodded. "Yes, I did. He's sweet."

"I hope you two will get married. As soon as I met you, I thought you were the one for him."

"Oh, thank you! That's so nice to hear."

"Be gentle with him," Linda cautioned. "He's the only one of my boys who's ever been in a serious relationship and had his heart broken. I thought for sure they'd marry."

Joy felt an overwhelming sense of jealousy, not even certain why. Whatever had happened was before she met him, so she had no reason or even any right to be jealous. "I wouldn't hurt him or anyone else. I promise."

Linda stood and hugged her. "I'm so glad you're going to be part of the family. Do you need any extra blankets or anything?"

Joy shook her head. "It's going to be strange to have my own room. I don't think that's ever happened to me. I've always shared with Chastity."

Lachele shook her head at that. "I'm sure that girl made interesting noises in the dark."

Joy blushed. "If she did, I never noticed." She put her glass into the dishwasher. "Good night. I'm so glad I'm going to be able to sleep alone for once, that I just can't express it."

Linda smiled as she watched her go. "That one seems more fragile than the others. I'm not sure why."

Lachele nodded. "I think you're right. I haven't gotten into her head yet, but I will. Probably not this weekend though."

"Do you have to leave already? You just got here!"

"I have a matchmaking business to run, and I still see clients in my mental health practice. Yes, I have to go. You know I'll be back to visit, though. It's so peaceful here. I miss living in Montana."

Linda shook her head. "I can't believe anyone would move from Montana to Manhattan. That's just crazy."

Lachele shrugged. "I thrive on the city pace, but I sure do love coming to the country every chance I get."

* * *

As soon as Joy got to her room, she took out her cell phone. It was seven, so it was nine at home in Kentucky. She hated that she was the one designated to call her parents, but they'd all known as they made the arrangements that she would be. It was always her job to deal with them, because she calmed them better than the others did.

She quickly punched in her mother's cell number and waited while it rang. It was answered on the second ring. "Joy? Where on earth are you?"

Joy sighed. She'd called her mother's phone, hoping for the less volatile of the two of them. "Hi, Daddy. We're in Wyoming."

"Wyoming? What are you doing there? What part of Wyoming? I'm on my way to get you!"

"No, you're not. Hope is already married, and Faith, Chastity, and I have men we're courting here. We saw a Christian matchmaker, and she set us up with four men."

"When did you see a matchmaker?"

Joy bit her lip, knowing now was the time to admit to everything. "Remember that weekend last month when we went into town to go to a friend's wedding?" They'd lied about the wedding, of course, and that had been another situation like this one, with Joy calling after they were already in town. She hated disappointing them.

"Yes…"

"There was no friend and no wedding. We met Dr. Lachele, and she set us up. We're here to marry four brothers." Joy closed her eyes, waiting for the yelling to start.

There was a long period of silence. "Why didn't you just tell us? You know your mother and I have been wanting you to get married for years."

"We weren't sure if you'd approve of us seeing a matchmaker." *In fact, we were sure you wouldn't.* "And we wanted to make you happy by marrying." *And there was no way we'd ever find husbands under your rule.*

There was more silence, and Joy could tell she'd upset him. "You'll let me know if something goes wrong and you need me?"

"Of course, we will!" Joy felt like she'd betrayed them when they'd just done everything they could to protect their children, but she knew they'd done the best thing for them.

"We love you, Joy. Tell your sisters we love them as well."

Joy felt a tear slip down her cheek. "We love you, too. Hug Mom and Grace and Honor for me!"

"Stay safe."

With those words, he ended the call, and Joy threw herself on her bed and sobbed. If he'd been mean and demanding, she would have been fine. The hurt in his voice had thrown her off.

There was a knock at the door, and Joy swiped the tears from her face, sitting up straight in bed. "Come in!"

Dr. Lachele's purple head stuck through the door. "You okay? I heard you talking."

Joy nodded. "I called my parents to let them know we'd arrived safely."

"Did you tell them you were coming here?" Dr. Lachele didn't wait for an invitation as she sprawled across Joy's bed.

"No, ma'am. We didn't. I thought they'd be angry, but my father was actually sweet. I was prepared for anger, but not love."

Dr. Lachele nodded. "Sometimes that's harder. Are you okay?"

Joy sniffled, another tear tracking down her cheek. "Mostly. I don't know why my parents turn me inside out like they do. They make all six of us crazy, but only I still have this intense feeling of loyalty toward them. I guess I'm crazier than they are."

"No, Joy. You just have a compassionate heart. That's a good thing." Dr. Lachele stood up and leaned down to press a kiss to Joy's forehead.

"Remember, anytime you need me, I'm just a phone call away. I have a feeling this is going to be tougher for you than any of the others."

Joy smiled at the older woman. "I'm sure I'll be fine, but thank you for caring so much."

"You'll keep my number handy, right?"

"Yes, ma'am. I have it programmed into my phone."

"Linda is a good one to talk to as well. She's going to be an incredible mother-in-law to you four girls."

Joy smiled. "I can see that already. Thank you."

Dr. Lachele closed the door softly behind her as she left the room, leaving Joy alone. Joy sighed. She was tired, but she wasn't sleepy. She pulled out her plastic canvas bag, and worked on her current project, a Barbie couch. If she was going to help save the Culpepper Ranch, she needed to keep stitching.

# Chapter 3

Joy woke early the next morning, her body still on Eastern Standard time. She wandered into the kitchen to find Linda making breakfast. "How can I help?" she asked, still wearing her pajamas.

Linda turned a smile on her. "Would you mind making the biscuits?"

"Not at all! Where's the flour?" Joy had made biscuits enough in her life that she had no problem whipping up a batch from the recipe in her memory.

"Flour? Oh, girl. Around here, we do everything the easy way. Can of Pillsbury is in the fridge."

Joy's eyes widened. "Pillsbury? What's that? And how can you have a can of biscuits?"

Linda stared at Joy as if she'd sprouted an extra four heads. "You've never had Pillsbury biscuits? You poor deprived child." She reached into the fridge and plucked the can of biscuits off the door. "Here. Just follow the instructions. Easy as pie."

Joy stared down at the long tube in her hand. "Where's the can opener?"

"Can opener?" Linda took the can back from Joy and efficiently peeled the label off before banging the tube twice on the counter.

When the can popped, Joy jumped a foot. "Is it supposed to do that?"

Linda nodded, her eyes full of laughter. "Well, yeah. Your mom really never made canned biscuits?"

Joy shook her head. "No, we always mixed the dough, and rolled them out, and then we used a biscuit cutter. I didn't know there was another way to do it."

"Tell me something, Joy. Do you like to spend six hours in the kitchen cooking every meal?"

Joy shook her head adamantly. "I don't mind cooking, but if it were easier, I'd take the easy way." At least she thought she would.

"Pillsbury is the easy way. You just pop open the can, removed the pre-cut biscuits, put them on a cookie sheet, and you bake them for the specified time. Doesn't get much easier than that."

"I feel like it's cheating." Joy did as she was told, separating the biscuits and putting them onto the cookie sheet. "Is this going to be enough for everyone?"

"Oh, good point. I don't even know if the boys are coming for breakfast. Make three cans."

Joy went to the fridge and took two more cans out, carefully peeling the labels off, as Linda had done. She jumped again when the cans popped. "It sounds like an explosion!"

Linda just laughed. "That's just how they work." She reached to the drawer under the stove and took out another cookie sheet. "Here. Go ahead and put them on both."

Joy did as she was told, carefully spacing out the biscuits. "Do you make cakes from box mixes and everything?"

"Duncan Hines and Betty Crocker are my best friends! Don't tell me you usually make cakes from scratch?" Linda looked appalled at the very idea.

"I do. I bake cookies from scratch too!"

"Oh, yeah, I always bake cookies from scratch. Then I can make them just how I want them." Linda turned back to the sausage she was frying. "I thought we could do biscuits and sausage gravy with scrambled eggs for breakfast. How does that sound?"

"Sounds good." Honestly, Joy had never had that for breakfast. Her mother had been a fanatic about healthy cooking. She could see there was some real adjusting she would need to do living there.

When she finished with the biscuits, Linda had her beat the eggs for the scrambled eggs. "I figure we'll just make enough for whoever shows up."

"Hope will come for breakfast," Joy told her.

"Don't you think Hope will make breakfast for Karlan and eat with him?"

"She usually will. Not today. She's going to come for breakfast so she can talk to us about our plan to save the ranch."

Linda turned to Joy. "You girls haven't had a chance to talk since Travis was here. How do you have a plan to save the ranch?"

Joy shrugged. "We just do. We've always had that intuition thing going that multiples have. As soon as Travis left, Hope gave me a look that let me know she'd be here this morning. We'll talk about it over breakfast, and we'll have a strong financial plan by noon."

"We?" Linda asked. "Are you girls taking on our financial problems as your own?"

"Of course, we are. That's what family does. And we're all about to be family. Hope is already your daughter-in-law, but Faith, Chastity, and I will be soon, too. We have to help."

Linda smiled brightly. "With nine of us working together, I'm sure we'll be able to make it work."

"I'm going to warn you now, Hope is going to drag you into whatever scheme she has up her sleeve. She's pretty bossy."

"That comes from being the oldest. I'm sure it will all work out perfectly."

Joy smiled as she set the beaten eggs on the counter. Yes, it would all work out perfectly. She was about to marry into a supportive family, and she couldn't wait.

* * *

Hope showed up just after they sat down for breakfast. It took all of ten minutes for her to explain her plan to everyone. Basically, each sister would work at her craft, and Hope would open a daycare in the big house, which they all would take turns helping with.

Joy's job for the daycare would be working during naptime and filling in wherever else she was needed. She was chosen for naptime because hers was a quiet craft.

Immediately after breakfast, Joy let her sisters help out with the dishes, since she'd helped with the cooking, and she wandered off to do some research on the internet. She needed to find the best way to sell her creations. She knew about Etsy and eBay, of course, but wondered if creating her own website would be smarter.

She worked in silence until there was a knock on her door. "Come in!" she called, looking up from her laptop.

Kolby walked into her room, closing the door behind him. He walked over and sat on the bed with her. "What are you working on?"

"I'm fine-tuning my part of the plan for helping save the ranch," she told him, thrilled he'd gone out of his way to search her out. She'd spent the night tossing and turning, wondering if she'd see him with Faith or Chastity today.

He nodded, deciding to humor her. Hopefully the women could help a little, but he wasn't going to count on much. He spotted a little couch on her nightstand and stood up, turning it over in his hand. "This is cool. Have you thought about selling these?"

Joy stared at him blankly for a moment. "What a great idea. I'll have to do that." She wasn't usually sarcastic, but there were times it was just necessary to get her point across.

He grinned. Maybe with this type of craftsmanship, she could help out with the ranch's finances. He sat back down, still holding the small couch. "How long did it take you to make this?"

She shrugged. "An hour or two. It only went that quick, because I've made that one multiple times."

He set it down. "Mom's got lunch almost ready. Are you hungry?"

"Yeah." She pushed her laptop off her lap and onto the bed beside her. "Are you done working for the day?"

Kolby nodded. "Karlan declared this afternoon his honeymoon, so the rest of us are taking the afternoon off as well. Cooper'll probably work, but that's only because it's on his schedule."

"Schedule?"

"Yeah, Cooper is nuts about his schedule. He won't deviate in any way. I think he's a little OCD."

Joy thought for a moment and remembered that Cooper and Faith had seemed to be getting along swimmingly. His brother Chris was the one who Chastity had set her sights on. "He seems nice enough."

"Oh, he's nice. All my brothers are good men. He's just kind of weird about time." He got to his feet and held a hand out to her pulling her to him. Leaning down, he kissed her softly. "G'morning, sunshine."

She wrapped her arms around his neck, kissing him back. "Did you have a good morning working?"

He shrugged. "We're working on fixing the last of the fences on the pasture we'll move the cattle to this week. So, not particularly."

"I'm sorry! I don't think I'd like that either."

He turned from her, opening the door. "Let's go eat. I'm starving."

He held her hand as they approached the table, noting that Cooper was fawning over Faith, and Chris looked like he was trying to find any flat surface to throw Chastity onto. "Lunch smells good, Mom."

Linda smiled. "Faith cooked."

"I guess that puts me on supper duty," Chastity said, breaking the kiss she was sharing with Chris.

Joy answered. "Sure does. Your turn."

Chastity trailed a finger down the front of Chris's shirt. "I sure hope you'll be here for supper..."

Chris grinned at Chastity, having eyes only for her.

Joy wanted to roll her eyes, but she'd done her share of kissing in the past twenty-four hours. Maybe not as much as Chastity had, but who could keep up with Chastity? She wondered if Chris had any idea what he was getting into.

Dr. Lachele looked at Chris and Chastity. "Do you two remember the contracts you've signed?"

"Yes'm," Chastity said demurely. Joy rolled her eyes at Kolby, squeezing his hand under the table.

"Oh, yes, ma'am. Nothing will happen before vows are spoken." Chris's voice didn't sound at all convincing.

Dr. Lachele glared at the two of them. "Make sure it doesn't."

After lunch, Joy went into the kitchen to help with the dishes, but Dr. Lachele shooed her away. "I'm going to help, so I can have a little more time with my friend before I leave. Go enjoy your man."

Joy blushed, looking over her shoulder at Kolby. Was he her man?

Kolby held out his hand for her. "Do you like to walk?"

She nodded. "Of course."

"Grab six bottles of water, and meet me out front in five minutes. Wear your most comfortable shoes."

Joy nodded, rushing into her room to put shoes on. Since she'd been in the house all day, she hadn't bothered. Shoes were for going outside, not for hanging around the house. She'd never understand why some women loved shoes so much. She hated them.

She put on a pair of sneakers and went to the kitchen. "Kolby said to get six bottles of water."

Linda nodded toward the fridge. "There's some in there. Do you need a bag to carry them in?"

Joy shrugged. "I don't know. Probably. He said we're going for a walk."

Linda frowned. "Wait here."

Joy dug the water out of the fridge while she waited for Linda who had disappeared.

Linda returned with a backpack. "This belonged to one of the boys when they were small." She handed it to Joy who put the bottles of water into it. Taking it back, she added a small first aid kit that was on top of the fridge, and several packs of peanut butter crackers. "That'll keep you."

"Do you really think we'll need all that?"

Linda shrugged. "With Kolby, you never can tell. He's unpredictable at times, and he loves to hike."

Joy took the backpack. "Thank you. I appreciate the help."

Linda smiled and hugged her. "Be safe and have fun."

"I'll try." Joy headed for the front door, finding Kolby waiting for her in his pick-up truck.

She opened the passenger door, and slid in beside him, immediately buckling her seat belt. She set the backpack on the seat between them. "Your mom added peanut butter crackers and a first aid kit."

He grinned. "That's my mom. She believes in being prepared for everything." He put the truck in reverse, and backed into the yard.

"Where are we going?" she asked.

"I thought we'd go there," he said nodding toward the mountain range in front of them.

"Climbing?" she asked, her eyes wide. She wasn't sure she was up to that.

"Not this time. There's a river at the base of the mountains, and we'll walk along the river. It's so peaceful there."

"That sounds nice."

Kolby smiled. "Trust me. It is. You're going to love Wyoming. It's one of the most beautiful places on earth."

"I just hope we can get used to driving in the snow in the winter." She had never even had her own car. Hope was given one when they started college, but she'd driven the others wherever they needed to go.

"I hadn't thought of that. With you girls being from the South, you haven't driven in snow much."

"We get some snow, but our father never let us drive in it. He didn't think women should ever drive in less than perfect conditions."

He rolled his eyes. "You'll have more freedom here. If you can't drive in snow, you can't drive."

Joy smiled at that. "I love the idea of having more freedom."

"It's strange to me the way you were raised. Why were your parents so strict?"

She sighed. "Mainly, it was a religious thing. We went to a very conservative church, and small Christian school. Our parents believed that women should have only one purpose in life and that was to be good wives and mothers. Until such a time as they married, they should be training for marriage."

"That's really sad. What if one of you wanted to be a doctor?"

"We weren't allowed. We all have college degrees, but we got them in homemaking. Hope has a minor in accounting, and Daddy almost came unglued when he found out what she'd done with her electives."

"Did you get a minor?" he asked.

She nodded. "Psychology."

"How did your parents feel about that?"

"They were fine with it when I told them I wanted to learn it to better choose a husband, and because I thought it would help me deal with my children in the future. Hope couldn't claim that with accounting."

He chuckled. "Good thinking."

She stared straight ahead at the beautiful mountains. "We're getting close," she whispered in awe.

He smiled. "I'm glad you like my mountains."

"I don't know how you can get any work done with them looming over you. I'd want to be here every day."

He turned off into a small parking lot. "This is as far as we can go by truck. The rest is walking." He snagged the back pack, putting it over one shoulder. "Let's go!"

Joy could see a walking trail beside the river, and she eagerly climbed out of the truck. "I do want to try to climb the mountain one day."

He grinned. "We'll have to get you some boots first. Those shoes will never work."

"I'd have gotten some if I'd realized how close we'd be to mountains." She stared up at the mountain closest, her eyes wide with wonder.

He took her hand, and led her to the path beside the river, walking at a leisurely pace. "This is my favorite place to come when I'm feeling down for any reason. The water speaks to me, and having the mountains so close doesn't hurt either."

"I can see that. It really is beautiful here. I wish I'd brought a blanket and a picnic lunch. This would be a perfect spot for it."

"I've done that here many times."

"Have you brought women here before?" she asked, not sure where the words came from. She really didn't want to know what he'd done with other girls.

He nodded. "Just one."

"I bet she was special."

"I thought so at one point." He thought of the engagement ring he'd bought her, and dismissed it again. He could sell it now to help pay off the ranch.

Joy waited for him to say more, but when he didn't she let it go. She needed him to want to tell her things like that. "Tell me about your grandfather." She'd heard all about the terms of the will, and was more than willing to have children to help out.

Kolby sighed. "He was a good man, and usually a fair man. That's why this will has thrown us off so badly. I mean, we knew he wanted us to all marry and have kids, but forcing it is kind of ridiculous."

"Was he close to your cousin Travis?"

It was all Kolby could do not to spit on the ground when his cousin's name was spoken. He was so mad at the idiot, he wanted to scream. "Not at all. I mean, Travis would spend every summer on the ranch. He and Karlan are the same age. All four of us would be out on the ranch busting our butts, and Travis would refuse to even ride a horse. He spent all summer in the house playing video games, and he complained about how desolate it was here. He has no right to any of the money from the ranch. None of it."

"Is he married?"

"Yes, and I think that's why Granddaddy was so good to him in the will. He's married and has a couple of kids, which Granddaddy wanted from all of us. Travis was the only one who listened." He shook his head. "But why Travis would be willing to bankrupt us all just so he could get his hands on immediate money, I don't know."

Joy squeezed his hand tightly. "I'm sorry he's being so awful about it. We're going to make it work though."

He looked at her with surprise. "You sound like you've made it your mission to help."

"Of course we have. My sisters and I really are going to make enough money to make a dent in what you owe. Hope, Faith, and I are going into town tomorrow to see about starting a daycare."

"A daycare?"

"Sure. An in-home daycare will bring in a lot. Hope will be running it with your mom's help. All of us will continue working on our crafts and we'll sell them. Trust me. We're going to make a difference." She didn't mention Faith's baby doll business and how profitable it already was, because she didn't want to betray Faith's secret. She knew her sister would eventually tell everyone, but it was her place to do so, not Joy's.

He smiled, not sure how much their little crafts could possibly help, but he was willing to humor her. "Thanks for being so willing."

"If we all marry into your family, the ranch will be our children's inheritance. Of course, we're going to help."

"I never thought of it that way."

"We knew when we came here we were expected to have babies straight off. We all love kids and want them to have the best future possible." She stopped walking. "Can we drink some of that water?"

He stopped, shrugging the backpack off his shoulder. "Sorry. I should have offered you a bottle before we started walking."

"No, it's fine. I'm just thirsty now." She took the proffered bottle and opened it, swallowing deeply. They had just reached a wide point in the river, and she wanted to go a bit closer. "Can we go down the bank?"

He nodded. "It's steep. Can you manage?"

"I'm sure I can." He led the way, and she followed closely behind. When they reached the bottom, she sat down on the bank of the river. "Do you think it's too cold to stick my feet in?"

He laughed. "It's April in Wyoming. I guarantee it's too cold to stick your feet in."

She sighed. "It looks so beautiful, and the sun feels warm."

"That river is fed by streams coming in from the mountains. It's going to be barely above freezing. Go ahead if you don't believe me, but you'll regret it."

She smiled at him. "I trust you."

He sat down beside her, putting an arm around her shoulders. "I'm glad you like it out here as much as I do. Rachelle hated it."

She looked at him. "Is Rachelle the girlfriend you brought here?" She wanted to ask if she was the one who had broken his heart, but she didn't want to reveal how much his mother had told her.

He nodded. "Yeah."

When he said nothing more, she let the subject drop. "Thank you for bringing me here. I'm glad you shared your special place."

He turned her face up to his. "You're really special, Joy."

She blushed, not sure what to say to that. No man had ever complimented her before. "I think you're special too."

He leaned down, kissing her, softly at first, and then more passionately. His hand moved to her waist, pulling her more firmly into him.

Her hands moved behind his back, feeling the strength of his muscles through his T-shirt. This was a man who worked long hard physical hours. His strength was obvious through the fabric of his shirt. She wanted to touch his bare skin, but she didn't know if she should. Well, she knew she shouldn't, but she didn't know if he felt like it was all right.

As soon as the thought struck her, she moved her hands to the hem of his shirt, and slowly up under it, stroking his bare back.

He let out a groan, letting her know that he didn't mind her touch at all.

Kolby felt Gizmo spring to life, and he mentally told him to calm down. *She's not ready for that yet, Giz. Her first kiss was yesterday.*

Gizmo tented against his jeans, making it perfectly clear he wasn't about to listen to reason.

He pushed her down in the grass, looming over her to kiss her more passionately, his chest pressing against her breasts. He was careful to keep his hands on safe ground, not wanting to frighten her.

Joy was startled to topple backwards, but it felt so good to have him pressing down on her. She brought one jean-clad knee up to rub against his thigh, wishing they could be closer.

"You're killing me!" he growled, finally pulling away from her.

Joy looked at him, shock on her face. "I didn't mean to hurt you!"

He sighed. "You didn't hurt me. Gizmo just got a little too carried away for comfort."

"Gizmo?"

"My—you know." He had no problem saying the actual word for it, but had a feeling she would be a little shocked.

"Why Gizmo?" she asked, surprised he had a name for it.

Kolby shrugged. "I don't know. Because Mom's word was tallywhacker, and I hated it."

She giggled. "Tallywhacker is interesting, but I agree. Gizmo sounds so much more dignified." She sat up and took a swig of her water. "I am sorry I got you so worked up."

"I started it." He sat for a moment staring out at the river. "When are you going to marry me?"

Joy felt her heart leap into her chest. "I don't know. When do you want to get married?"

"Gizmo is screaming for ten minutes ago. Think we can make that happen?"

She shook her head. "How about in a week? Monday of next week."

He frowned. "Why do you want to get married on a Monday? Don't most people get married on a weekend?"

She shrugged. "They do. I think Mondays get too much hate. This way, a day that is normally dreaded will be a reason to rejoice. It will make people happy."

"Will it make you happy?"

Joy nodded emphatically. "Of course it will."

"Then we'll get married a week from tomorrow." He hugged her close. "Gizmo and I will be counting down the hours."

Joy blushed at that. "Can Gizmo count?"

"Not exactly, but I'll help him out. We *are* buddies after all."

"Of course you are." She slid close to him on the grass and kissed him again. "I thought we should do that one more time to seal our engagement." Her mind was already on wedding preparations. She and Hope were the same size, so she could wear her dress.

He could see she was thinking of something else, so he stayed quiet for a bit. "We should probably get back," he finally said. "Mom and Dr. Lachele will think I brought you out here and ravaged you."

"I'll tell them you didn't." She stood up, brushing the grass off her bottom. "It's going to be a long week."

"That's what Gizmo keeps telling me. Are you sure you don't want to do it tomorrow?"

She nodded. "I need a little bit. I was kissed for the first time yesterday. I want to enjoy being engaged for a week."

He shrugged. "I guess we can live with that."

Joy smiled, standing on tiptoe to kiss him again. "I sure hope so."

# Chapter 4

As the week flew by, Joy worked alongside her sisters, both in the daycare and making her crafts. She enjoyed getting to know Linda, and had some private time with Kolby every evening. Not nearly enough time with Kolby to suit her, but she understood they both had jobs to do.

After attending Faith and Cooper's wedding on Saturday, Kolby took Joy for a drive, still dressed in their wedding finery. He surprised her by stopping at a small lake and getting out of the car.

"What are we doing here?" she asked. She looked down at her shoes, which were not meant for walking any kind of distance.

"Having dinner." He got out of the truck and came around, opening her door for her, holding her hand to help her down. "Those heels look like they're tough to maneuver in."

Smiling, she happily let him assist her. She'd never been what she considered a "modern woman." She liked old-fashioned values. "Thank you."

"My pleasure." He hurried to the back of the truck and pulled out a quilt and a picnic blanket. "It's a little chilly, but I promise to keep you warm."

Joy felt a trickle of pleasure settle in her stomach. This man—she already loved him. Yes, she'd only known him for a week, but he was kind and caring. She couldn't wait to start their lives together.

He spread the blanket out, and she dug into the picnic basket. He'd made sandwiches and stuck a bag of potato chips in the hamper. She grinned as she saw it. There were some bottles of water as well. "It's perfect." She removed the paper plates and added a sandwich to each.

"What did you think of the wedding?"

Joy giggled. "I love Brother Anthony. Have you talked to him about marrying us yet?"

"He's agreed to do it. Do you want to marry at the big house like Hope and Karlan? Or at the church like Faith and Cooper?"

"I think I want to marry outside. Like in your mom's backyard. Do you think she'd mind?"

Kolby laughed. "Mind? When she's going to be getting grandkids? No, I don't think she'll mind. You could tell her you wanted to have the ceremony in her bathroom, and she'd just go about seeing how she could make it work."

Joy blushed at the mention of grandkids. It felt so strange to think they'd be making love in just a couple of days. "How many kids do you want?" she asked. "We haven't even discussed that."

He shrugged. "No idea. I don't know that I've ever really thought about it."

"Well, you should think about it. What if I want fifteen children? You know...there's always the chance I'll have 'litters' like my mom did." She looked down, disgusted by the word that had often been used to describe she and her sisters.

"How would you feel about having more than one baby at a time?" He was a bit startled at the prospect, but it made sense. He'd prefer one at a time, but he'd take what he could get.

"I don't know. I know multiples are a lot of work. My mom had shifts of women from the church helping around the clock." She shook her head. "I don't think I'd mind twins, but four at once is a bit of a handful."

He thought over her words as they ate. "You'd have help if that happened. My mom would be thrilled. She'd have had a lot more kids if she hadn't lost Dad so young."

"I can see that. She's certainly welcomed my sisters and me with open arms. I don't think I've ever felt so included as I have with your family."

"I'm glad." He took a swig of water out of the bottle in his hands. "I'm glad we're getting married." His eyes studied her in the waning light of evening. Everything about her was beautiful. He'd have to be more careful around her. His heart needed to stay strong enough to keep her out of it.

Joy nodded, blushing a little. "So am I." She wanted to tell him she loved him, but she wasn't sure if the time was right.

When she'd finished eating, he stood, holding both hands down to help her to her feet. She'd been sitting with her legs curled discreetly to one side, because she was wearing a skirt. Taking his hands, she gracefully got to her feet, looking into his eyes. "Can you walk a little way in those shoes?"

She nodded. "I think so." Truthfully, her feet already ached a little, but she was willing to go wherever he wanted her to go.

With his arm around her waist, he led her to a huge rock about a five-minute walk from their picnic spot. "No one will steal your stuff?" she asked, looking back over her shoulder.

"Nah. We won't be here long enough. I thought you'd like to watch the sunset over the lake."

She sat carefully on the rock, not wanting to snag her dress. She had at least one more wedding to wear it to. Chastity and Chris had to be getting married soon, although they hadn't made any announcements yet.

He sat beside her, pulling her against him. She shivered delicately, so he shrugged out of his jacket and put it around her shoulders. "I think the sunset will be worth the chill."

She leaned against him with a smile. "The chill's a good excuse to snuggle. I'm never going to turn that down."

He kissed the top of the head resting against his shoulder. He was starting to have feelings for her, and he didn't like that much. He'd talk to her about it. Soon. She had a right to know he'd never love her.

As the sun slowly eased down over the mountains framing the lake, she let out a sigh of contentment. She was marrying a man she loved.

No longer living under her parents' roof. And it was the most beautiful place on God's green earth. What more could she ask for?

After the sunset, they walked back to the quilt they'd had their picnic on, and worked together to put everything back into the picnic basket. "You're awfully quiet," she said. He'd said almost nothing since they'd sat down to watch the sunset together. "Is everything all right?"

He nodded. "I just watched a gorgeous sunset with my beautiful fiancée. What could be wrong?" What worried him about his words was that he meant them with his whole heart. Was he falling in love with her? If he was, she could never know.

He helped her into the truck and ran around to the other side, climbing in. She was still wearing his black suit jacket, and to him, she was the most beautiful sight on earth. Her long curly red hair spilled down over her shoulders, and her petite body huddled into his jacket.

Without thinking through what he was doing, he unbuckled her seatbelt. "C'mere, you."

She slid across the seat to meet him in the middle, the gearshift keeping her from getting too close.

He slid the rest of the way, his arm going around her shoulders. He looked down into her eyes, caressing her cheek. "Have I mentioned how beautiful you are?"

She smiled, her green eyes sparkling. "Not nearly often enough. Have I mentioned how incredibly sexy I find you?"

"Sexy, huh?"

"Oh, yeah." She put her hand at the back of his neck and pulled his lips down to meet hers. They had taken walks and kissed every night that week, but every time she felt his lips against hers still sent a thrill through her body. Every time he touched her, she felt like her body was going to go up in flames. He was a special man, and she was so glad he was going to be hers forever.

He kissed her with the passion he'd been trying to suppress all week. They had so little time in the evenings after dinner with the whole family to just be together. He gathered her closer, crushing her against him. "Do we have to wait?"

Joy pulled away, frowning a little. "Honestly, I don't want to, but I've already compromised my morals enough just by kissing you before marriage. I don't think it would be right if we—did more."

He sighed, resting his forehead against hers. "Then Gizmo is going to insist we stop now. I want to kiss you forever. I want to take that blanket and spread it back out and lay you down, making slow sweet love with you."

She shuddered, seeing in her mind what he was saying. She could picture him lying over her, kissing her. "I'm sorry."

He shook his head. "There's no need to be sorry. We signed a contract stating we wouldn't do anything before marriage. Gizmo refused to sign, though. So he wanted to have his say."

"It was kind of you to speak for him."

Kolby shrugged. "That's just the kind of guy I am. Faithful to a fault."

"Obviously." She grinned up at him. "Only two more days, and I'll be Mrs. Kolby Culpepper."

"And I'll be filled with joy. Or Joy will be filled with Gizmo. Preferably both."

She gasped at his words, playfully swatting his shoulder. "You shouldn't say things like that!"

"You're going to be my wife in less than forty-eight hours. I can say just about anything at this point." He kissed her one last time before pushing her away. "Buckle up. We need to head home so I can return you to your chaperone."

"I wish we could stay here kissing all night," Joy said as she reluctantly did as she was told.

"Monday night we will kiss all night. I promise." He winked at her before starting the truck. "I can't wait until you're mine."

She thought about telling him they could move up the wedding to Sunday afternoon, but really, she wanted the extra day. She loved him, but she needed a little more time before she was ready to make love with him. She didn't know why, but it still felt like it was wrong.

He parked the truck in front of the big house, helping her down. Linda was sitting in the living room reading a book. "How was your picnic?"

"It was lovely. We watched the sun set over the mountains." Joy walked over to sit beside Linda, eager to talk about it all.

Kolby looked down at her, wondering at her quick abandonment of him for his mother. He walked around to sit beside her, deciding to be part of the conversation, at least for a few minutes. "She loves Wyoming almost as much as I do."

Linda smiled. "Of all my boys, you've always been the one who loves the mountains here the most."

"You don't love the mountains?" Joy asked with surprise.

"Oh, I do! I just wasn't raised here. Texas is still in my blood. Sometimes I think I should move back, but I have no one there anymore. No, I belong here with my boys and my mountains."

"And soon your grandbabies," Kolby pointed out, his arm around Joy's shoulders.

Joy blushed, not really wanting to talk about grandbabies with her future mother-in-law.

Linda nodded emphatically. "I'll take three dozen of those, please."

Kolby laughed. "I don't know. Joy wants fifteen of her own. That would be more like five dozen, wouldn't it?"

"I'll take five dozen! No problem!"

Joy smiled, leaning into Kolby, wishing he'd change the subject. "The wedding was beautiful."

Kolby laughed. "I think that's my cue she wants me to shut up. I'll go now." Then he turned her face to him, and kissed her, right there in front of Linda. She was so embarrassed, but she wasn't about to push him away.

"I'll see you after work tomorrow. We've been doing half days on Sundays."

She nodded. "Is it okay if we spend a little time at your house? I'd like to do an inventory of food and general cooking supplies, so I know what I need."

"Sure."

"And...this is going to sound weird, but I'd like to Skype with my parents tomorrow. I want you to 'meet' them before the wedding."

Kolby nodded. "I can do that." He honestly hated the idea. He'd heard enough about her parents from her, and what his brothers had heard from her sisters, that he wanted nothing to do with them, but he'd honor her, and do what she requested. Kissing her softly, he got to his feet. "See you tomorrow afternoon."

After he was gone, she turned to Linda again. "You did good with him."

Linda smiled. "I did good with all four of my boys. They're so different from each other, but they're good men."

"I think so," Joy said with a smile. "I want a quick finger food reception like Hope had, if that's okay. Nothing much."

Linda nodded. "Sounds good. I'll make a small wedding cake as well. Where do you want to have the wedding?"

"In the yard, if you don't mind. Kolby said you wouldn't."

"Not at all! It'll be nice to get the backdrop of the mountains in the wedding pictures."

"How on earth do you get anything done? I want to stand there and look at the mountains all day. I have no desire to work while I'm here."

Linda laughed. "Years of practice. When the boys were small, and I was keeping this house for my father-in-law, there was no time for anything but work. Now that there is, I find that I'm used to working."

"That makes sense." Joy stretched, kicking her shoes off and tucking her feet under her. "Tell me about Rachelle."

"He told you something about her?"

"Not much. I know her name, and I know she was an old girlfriend. What happened there?"

Linda shrugged. "I don't know a lot, and I don't know if what I do know is something I should repeat. I will say she broke his heart. It's the only heartbreak any of the four have ever had, and he was angry and miserable for a good long while. I think he's ready to move on." She frowned. "I'll add that I never liked her. She wasn't right for him, even though he thought she was. I'm glad she's out of the picture, because you're the right woman for my Kolby."

Joy smiled at the words. "Thank you for welcoming us so warmly. It's nice to be accepted for who we are."

"You girls fill my heart with joy. I'm glad you're here. And I'm glad you're the one for Kolby. I'm not sure your sisters could handle him."

Joy hugged Linda and got to her feet, bending down to pick up her shoes. "I'm getting married in my bare feet, and I don't care who protests."

Linda laughed. "That works."

"G'night!"

Joy wandered off to her room, sitting on her bed. Glancing at the clock, she saw it was after nine. With the two-hour time difference, it was too late to call her parents to let them know Faith was married, and that she would be married on Monday. She'd tell them when she skyped the next day.

Instead she sent a text message to her mother's phone, knowing her mom would have her phone off while she slept. "Skyping you tomorrow at nine your time. Much love."

Setting her phone on her nightstand, she brushed her teeth, and climbed into bed. Her mind was spinning. In two days, she'd be married to the sexiest man she'd ever met. The man she loved.

* * *

On Sunday morning, Joy woke early and headed into town to go to church. She asked Chastity to attend with her, but Chastity had been out late with Chris, and didn't seem to have any desire to go.

The sermon from Brother Anthony was so different than any she'd ever heard at home. At one point in the middle of his talk on the love of Christ and what he did for his followers, he lost his place. After peering at the page in front of him for a moment, he called out to his wife in the front row. "Lovie? I lost my place!"

Lovie, a gray-haired, always-smiling, slightly more than a little past middle-aged woman, hurried onto the stage and looked at his notes for him. "You're right there, Tony. Read the scripture from John next!"

"Yes, Lovie," he said, smiling at her as she hurried off the stage.

Looking around her, Joy could see no one even batting an eye, and she assumed Brother Anthony's shenanigans were common-place.

After church, people surrounded her, introducing themselves. Lovie hurried over and took over. "Oh, Joy, I want you to meet my grandson, Marcus. I hear you have two sisters still at home. They should come out here and meet my Marcus."

Joy blinked a couple of times, a slow grin spreading across her face. "That's a lovely idea. What do you do, Marcus?"

Marcus frowned at his grandmother. "I'm a lawyer."

"You are? What kind of law do you specialize in?"

He shrugged. "I don't do criminal cases, but I do pretty much everything else."

"I may ask you to look over a will. Would you be willing to do that?"

"Only if I don't have to marry one of your little sisters as payment."

Joy choked on a laugh. "I think you'd love my sisters, but whatever. Would you be willing to read it?"

Marcus nodded slowly. "Maybe we could have lunch, and you could show it to me?"

"Oh, I can't." She glanced down at her phone for the time. "My fiancé and I are having lunch together at noon. I need to get back out to the ranch."

Marcus frowned. "Fiancé?"

"I'm marrying Kolby Culpepper tomorrow," Joy said with a grin.

"He's a good man. I can see when I'm beat. Maybe I'll meet one of your sisters after all."

Joy laughed and shook her head. "I'm trying to get them out here, so maybe we'll make that happen."

"All right."

"I'll have Kolby talk to you about the will. Does that work?"

"Yeah, that's fine. He's got my number."

Joy squeezed his hand. "Thanks so much!"

She hurried out the church after that, ignoring the long line of men who had been waiting to meet her. When she got back to the ranch, she parked Linda's SUV in the driveway and hurried into the house to change before lunch. She liked the freedom to wear jeans she had in Wyoming.

When she was dressed, she went out to find Linda and Chastity making lunch together. "I'm jealous that Chastity will have you all to herself after tomorrow."

"That's why she'll always love me best," Chastity said, sticking her tongue out at her sister.

"I really do worry about you sometimes, Chastity."

"You and the rest of the world."

Joy shook her head, but took the plates that were on the counter and set the table for five. The assumption was that Hope and Faith would eat with their husbands.

Linda only seemed to use paper plates. When Joy had questioned it, Linda had responded that she had better things to do than stand around doing dishes all day. It seemed to be like the biscuit thing. She was going to make life just as easy on herself as she could.

Joy had just finished setting the table when the back door opened. Kolby had obviously taken the time to shower after work, because he was dressed in clean jeans and a skin-tight T-shirt. Joy's eyes traveled over him, liking what she saw. She walked to him and kissed him, forgetting there were other people there. Her hands were flat on his chest, and she kissed him with all of the passion pent up inside her.

Kolby kissed her back, finally breaking away after a moment. "Much more of that, and Gizmo is going to insist I take you home and forget all about the fact there's no marriage certificate," he whispered against her ear.

Joy blushed, stepping back. The back door opened again, and Chastity ran to Chris throwing her arms around his neck and kissing him.

Joy rolled her eyes at the spectacle her sister was making of herself, and then she stopped. She'd done the same thing just moments before. She had no room to judge.

# Chapter 5

After lunch, Kolby took Joy to his house, and she rummaged around in his kitchen, making notes on her iPhone as she did. She made a list of things she needed to purchase.

Kolby leaned against the counter and watched her. Finally, she turned to him. "You have almost nothing to cook with here."

"I usually just eat at Mom's. She's lonely."

"She's lonely, or you don't feel like ever cooking for yourself?" Joy asked.

He walked into the kitchen putting his arms around her. "Well, you can interpret that how you want." He kissed her softly. "Tomorrow night, I'm keeping you here."

She smiled, stroking his cheek. "That's the plan."

He groaned, staring into her green eyes. "You know...I think we should head to town. I don't know that being alone is good for us." And Gizmo was already starting to protest.

She laughed. "Let's go then."

They went out to the truck, and while they drove, she told him about church that morning. "Marcus said you should call him, and he'll read over the will for you."

"Why would he do that?" Marcus had never gotten along well with the Culpeppers. He'd been in Chris's year at school, and he had always been jealous of the Culpepper's success with girls.

"I offered to set him up with one of my sisters."

Kolby let out a bark of laughter. "That man has always coveted the Culpepper women. Did he ask you out?"

Joy blushed. "Not exactly."

"He did! I knew it! Well, if he's willing to read over the will for the chance to be set up with one of your sisters, that works for me."

They ran into several people Kolby knew at the grocery store, and he introduced Joy to each of them as his fiancée. "Do you know everyone in town?" she asked as they walked away from his old high school principal.

"Of course, I do. Karlan is the mayor of this town, and it was named after one of our ancestors. Colonel Culpepper was one of the first settlers in this area."

"I'll have to find a book about him. He sounds interesting."

"Oh, he is. We studied him in school."

They walked to the checkout with Joy's huge cart full of stuff. "I'm going to order the pots and pans I need online. I think it'll be cheaper than finding them here."

He nodded. "Almost always."

The woman at the checkout squealed when she saw Kolby. "It's been ages!"

Kolby nodded. "How are things with you?"

"Good. Just got back from California. We were visiting Rachelle and Neville. The baby is adorable."

"I hope you had a great time."

"Oh, I did. She asked about you."

Kolby looked at Joy. "I'm sorry, sweetheart. I didn't mean to be rude. This is Abigail. She's the sister of an old girlfriend. Abigail, this is my fiancée, Joy."

Joy smiled sweetly at the girl, feeling hurt that the first time he'd used an endearment with her, it had been because of his ex-girlfriend's sister. "It's nice to meet you, Abigail."

"Engaged! I heard a couple of your brothers got married. You too? I thought you'd never marry after Rachelle..." She trailed off, glancing at Joy. "I hope you two will be very happy together."

"We will. She's an incredible Christian woman with strong morals. Thank Rachelle for me the next time you see her." He paid for the groceries and headed for the exit of the store.

He was moving so quickly, Joy had to practically run to keep up. "What was that about?"

He shrugged. "Nothing. I was ready to get out of there. You know I prefer being outside."

She stood awkwardly, wishing she knew what had happened. Once they were in the truck, she tried one more time. "Will you tell me what happened with Rachelle?"

He shrugged. "It wasn't a big deal. We were dating, and I thought things were more serious than they were. A ranch on the other side of town had a photoshoot for male underwear models. When the women in town found out there were sexy men, they all ran to volunteer to help. There was a freak April blizzard, and they were trapped on the ranch for four days. Lots of weddings happened right after that. Rachelle's was one of them."

Joy blinked a couple of times. What did he mean he'd thought things were more serious than they were? "Were you engaged?"

He shook his head. "Nope. Not engaged." He put the truck in reverse and pulled out of the parking spot. Within a minute or two, they were on the road, heading back toward the ranch.

"Do you still love her?" Joy asked, her voice soft.

"I honestly don't think I ever did. Sure, I thought so at the time, but I couldn't love someone who was so wrong for me, could I?" He wished she'd drop the subject, but he didn't know how to tell her to leave it alone.

Joy frowned, staring out the window. She was in love with him, and he didn't seem to be over his ex-girlfriend. Not really the way she'd wanted to start her marriage.

Instead of talking more, Kolby reached out and turned the radio up on his truck. The words of an old cheating country song filled the truck. It seemed appropriate, so he left it there.

When they reached the ranch, he drove to his house, and carried in groceries while she put things away. His cupboards had been bare, so she was setting up her own system of organization, certain he wouldn't care. She knew she was marrying a man who would expect her to bring him food and drink when he was hungry and thirsty. She'd never expected anything else from her life.

"Why don't I fix us dinner tonight? If you'd like, that is. I texted my parents and told them we'd Skype them around nine their time, which is seven here."

He nodded, seeming distracted. While she went about the business of cooking for them, he turned the television on, becoming involved in a baseball game.

Joy wanted to know how to end the coldness between them, but she really had no idea.

While the casserole she'd prepared was in the oven, she walked over to sit beside him on the couch. Instead of cuddling against him as she usually would, she left an entire couch cushion between them. "You don't have to marry me if you don't want to."

Kolby muted the television with the remote in his hand and turned to her. "I do want to marry you, but I think you know as well as I do that our marriage isn't for normal reasons."

She nodded, swallowing hard. "I know it's not."

"I have a lot of feelings for you, Joy, but they're not feelings of love. I want you. I want to spend every night making love with you. I like the idea of having children with you. But love doesn't enter into it, and I don't know if it ever will. I would prefer if it didn't, to be honest." His gaze was steady and his face serious. He didn't want to hurt her, and he needed to be brutally honest with her to spare her any pain.

Joy felt her heart shatter as she nodded, meeting his eyes. "I understand." But she didn't. Of course, she didn't. How could she?

"I'm glad." He reached out and squeezed her hand, trying to take the sting from his words. He was glad they'd discussed everything.

She watched him for a moment, wondering how she could go on. Would she be able to have sex with a man who didn't love her? She sighed. She'd have to, wouldn't she? She'd come out there unsure if she'd find love through Dr. Lachele's machinations. Just because she'd found it so quickly didn't mean that Kolby was required to.

"Are you angry with me?" he asked finally, after she'd sat silently for what seemed like hours, but was really only a minute or two.

Joy shook her head. "Honestly, I'm a little hurt. I'm not sure how I feel about marrying someone who told me he never wants to love me."

"Are you calling it off? I guess you could always talk to Chris—if you can pry Chastity's lips off him, that is." He was disgusted at the idea of her marrying his brother, but he couldn't keep her tied to him if it was just going to make her unhappy.

"Is that what you want?" she asked, her voice calm. Did he really care that little?

He shook his head. "No. I picked the girl I wanted that first night. I'm very attracted to you. I want to spend my life with you."

Joy tilted her head to one side, trying to understand him. "So you're attracted to me. You want to spend your life with me. You want to make love with me. You want to have children with me. But you never want to love me. How does that even make sense?"

Kolby sighed. "I guess it doesn't make a lot of sense, but it's how I feel."

"All right. I guess I'll just have to live with that then, won't I?" She would never make a play for her sister's man. It wasn't in her. Besides, she was marrying the man she loved. Having her love returned would be perfect, but life was rarely perfect.

After supper, she put the dishes in the dishwasher and reached for her iPad, moving over to sit beside him on the couch. "Are you ready to Skype?" she asked.

He nodded, not wanting to do it, but knowing he would do anything for her after the way he'd hurt her earlier. He'd seen the sadness in the eyes that were usually filled with happiness. Taking her hand in his, he squeezed it tightly.

"I want them to think we're in love," she whispered softly. "Please don't shame me in front of my parents."

He put his arm around her and kissed her cheek. "I do care for you, Joy. I would never do that. Everyone in the world will think we're madly in love, if that's what you want."

She nodded. "That's what I want." She couldn't be joyful otherwise. "Ready?"

He took one corner of the iPad, and she held the other. Pushing the icon to call, she held his hand tightly again.

Tears pricked Joy's eyes when her parents' faces jumped onto the screen. "Hi, Mom. Hi, Dad. This is Kolby. We're getting married tomorrow."

Her mother's eyes swam with tears. "That doesn't give us any time at all to get there."

"It's not going to be a formal wedding. Just something in Kolby's mother's backyard. Faith got married yesterday."

"And Chastity? Is she still doing everything she can not to live up to her name?" her mother asked, her eyes chilly.

"Chastity and my brother are talking marriage," Kolby said, having no idea if his words were true. As far as he knew, they were just going at each other like rabbits, but he wouldn't betray his brother or her sister by saying so.

Joy's father frowned at him. "What do you do for a living?"

"My brothers and I share a ranch. We're all hard-working cowboys." He didn't mention Chris's true vocation. Why would he admit to having a science teacher for a brother?

"I see." The older man nodded. "Nothing wrong with good old-fashioned hard work."

"No, sir. There's not." Kolby didn't particularly like the man, but he wasn't about to be rude. He'd been raised better than that.

Joy smiled, her eyes lit up. "I just wanted to let you meet Kolby before the wedding. This seemed like the best way."

Joy's mother cried a bit. "I hate that I can't be there for your wedding. At least you told us before you actually married him, though."

"I did what I felt was right, Mama. The others did too."

"I see."

"I'm going to let you go. I just wanted you to know that we're all happy, and I'm getting married tomorrow."

Joy's father looked at Joy for a moment. "Are we going to be able to see our grandchildren?" he asked.

Joy bit her lip, not sure how to answer that.

"Yes, of course you'll be able to see them," Kolby answered, understanding Joy's hesitation. *You'll see them under supervision and you'll never take them home with you.*

Her father nodded. "Thank you. Take good care of my Joy."

The screen went dark, and Joy felt tears streaming down her cheeks. "I feel so bad for the way we ran off, but we didn't feel like we had a choice. I felt so stifled under their roof, but it was worse for the others."

Kolby laid the iPad on an end table and pulled her into his arms, stroking her back while she cried on his shoulder. "Do you want to go home?" he asked, hating the idea, but knowing he'd let her go if that's what would make her happy.

She shook her head. "Back to Kentucky? No, I want to stay here with you. It's just hard to let them be angry with me."

"How are you going to get your sisters away from them?" he asked.

She shrugged. "Grace has a car. Those two will just pack up and leave. They helped us a lot by distracting Mom and Dad while we were packing."

"You just left, didn't you? You snuck around and left without them knowing about it."

Joy leaned back, looking him in the eye. "It's the only way we could get out of there unless we'd married men our father hand-picked."

He sighed. "I'm sorry you had to go through that."

She shrugged. "They love us a great deal. They just show love differently than most people do."

"Are you glad we talked to them?"

"I think so. At least I won't have to feel guilty about marrying you without introducing you to them first."

He frowned, seeing that her eyes were still sad. "What can I do to make you feel better?"

She smiled. "Why don't you walk me back to your mom's house? I still have a few things I need to do tonight so I'm ready to get married tomorrow."

"I'm going to take Tuesday off work. My brothers are both nuts about schedules and working, but I'm taking a day with my new bride." He got to his feet, holding his hand down for her. "C'mon. I'll walk you back."

He picked up her iPad, and holding her hand tightly in his, began the short walk back to his mother's house. "Can you take off the whole day Tuesday?"

She frowned. "I'm really not sure. Hope would let me if I asked, but I'd feel guilty."

"Why? She's going to have a day soon where she'll take a day off as well. You'll cover for each other."

"Neither of the others took the day after they married off. I feel like I'd be taking advantage if I did."

Kolby sighed. "Have you ever thought of yourself first? Even once in your life?"

Joy shook her head. "My mom taught me that Joy means Jesus first, others second, and yourself last. I need to exhibit joy, so I make sure I follow the formula to do so."

He stopped walking for a moment and turned to her in the dark. "I hope you don't burn yourself out by constantly doing for others."

She smiled, standing on tiptoe to brush his lips with hers. "I won't."

He caught her by the hips and pulled her closer, his mouth coming down hard on hers. He wanted so badly to drag her back to his place. What would it hurt to anticipate their wedding vows by less than twenty-four hours?

He stopped, pulling away slowly. It would hurt her. He may not be willing to love her, but he wouldn't hurt her! "Let's get you back." He rested his forehead against hers, breathing heavily. "I can't wait for tomorrow night."

She raked her fingers through his hair. "I can't either." She knew she shouldn't be so eager to marry a man who never planned to love her, but she was. She loved him, and she would be happy with him. She could live without his love.

He smiled, keeping his arm around her shoulders as he walked the rest of the way back to his mother's house. Opening the back door, he called out, "I brought your little chick back to you safely!"

Linda walked over from where she'd been standing beside the dining room table sewing. "It's the last time you'll need to bring her back to me."

Kolby looked at Joy with a grin. "I'm happy about that."

"Are you going to be here for lunch tomorrow?" Linda asked her son.

He nodded. "I plan to be. I'll get ready for the wedding immediately after work. Do you two have everything worked out the way you want it?"

Joy nodded, a smile on her face. "Yes, of course. I have already chosen flowers, and they'll be delivered. Brother Anthony and Lovie will be here at seven. All we have to do is show up."

"Well, you sleep well." He kissed her cheek, his lips touching her ear. "I can't promise you're going to get a lot of sleep tomorrow night."

She blushed, glancing over at Linda to make certain she hadn't heard. "G'night." Joy watched him go before turning to Linda. "I met Rachelle's sister today."

"Abigail? She's sweet. She and Karlan were in the same grade in school." Linda kept methodically cutting strips of fabric for the baby doll quilts. "Did she say anything?"

"She told Kolby that they'd just returned from seeing Rachelle and her husband in California. Mentioned a baby. Kolby completely shut down."

"I'm sure he did. Did he tell you what happened?"

"Yeah. She was part of the Great Underwear Model Caper." Joy made a disgusted face.

Linda laughed. "Yes, she was. Trust me, Joy, that woman was not worthy of one of my boys. She had him wrapped around her little finger, and he would have done anything for her. Instead, she ran off looking for trouble. Did he tell you she called him when she was five months pregnant, begging him to take her back?"

Joy shook her head, her eyes wide.

"Well, she did. He told her he wanted nothing more to do with her, and she'd made her bed, so it was time to lie in it. That told me everything I need to know."

"That Kolby can't forgive?"

"No, Kolby forgives easily. It told me that he never loved her like he thought he did."

"Are you sure?" Joy needed to believe that Kolby really hadn't loved her, because that meant that his heart wasn't broken, and maybe eventually he would love Joy.

"Of course, I'm sure! I wouldn't say it if I wasn't." Linda shook her head. "You need to not worry about Rachelle. You're five times the woman she was."

Joy laughed. "Sure. I have a feeling Kolby doesn't feel that way."

"He didn't take her back, and he would have if there had ever been real love on his side. Keep that in mind."

Joy nodded, walking around to the kitchen to get a glass of water. "I'll try. I sure don't want to spend the rest of my life feeling like I'm living in the woman's shadow."

"Then don't let yourself. She's gone. You're his future. He wouldn't marry you if he didn't think he could be happy with you."

"Thanks for the pep talk. Now if I can just make it through the day tomorrow without losing my mind with nervousness."

Linda laughed. "You're going to be just fine."

"G'night." Joy put the glass in the dishwasher and headed off to her room, just then realizing it was her last night to sleep there. Only Chastity would be left.

Climbing into bed, she set her alarm. Mornings came early on the ranch. She prayed for peace and calm the following day. Adding at the end, "And please, God, let Kolby love me. I need him to."

# Chapter 6

When Joy woke at five-thirty on Monday morning, her first thought was of her conversation with Kolby the previous evening. *I'm going to marry him anyway, and I'm going to help him see that loving me is the only thing he can do.*

She hurried through her shower, planning a long leisurely bath that afternoon. She was going to get dressed like this wedding was the most important day of her life, because it was. No matter what Kolby said, she was marrying him because she loved him. How could that ever be a bad thing?

She went out to eat breakfast with Chastity and Linda before the children came. When she entered the kitchen, Linda smiled at her. "It's our bride. Are you ready for this?"

Joy nodded, taking a deep breath and plastering her smile on her face. "I think I am. Kolby is a wonderful man, and I'm excited to be able to spend my life with him."

She grabbed a bowl of cereal and sat down opposite Chastity. "How are you this morning?"

Chastity smiled. "Mostly good. Are you excited about the wedding?"

Joy nodded. "Of course. How could I not be?" Her signature smile was on her face, and she knew her sister wouldn't see through it. Everyone was used to her always smiling, so they never saw through it.

When Hope arrived for work, she brought her wedding dress with her, giving it to Joy. "I bet you thought I'd forget, didn't you?"

Joy shook her head. "I knew you'd remember."

"I didn't bring my shoes, because I knew they wouldn't fit you. What are you doing for shoes?"

"I'm getting married in my bare feet."

Hope laughed. "I love that. You totally should. You've always been a shoe hater."

Joy nodded. "Since birth." She looked at Linda, who didn't understand the joke. "When we were babies, we all looked a whole lot alike. So looking back at baby pictures, there are signs that tell us apart. Hope always had one little curl on top of her forehead that wouldn't go away. Faith always had her finger up her nose. Chastity always had a smudge of dirt on her cheek. I always took my shoes off. Always. Mom said she could never keep them on me for more than a minute or two at a time."

Linda laughed. "I haven't seen a single smudge of dirt on Chastity's cheek since she got here!"

"But did you know to look?" Joy asked, and they all laughed.

Chastity sighed. "I'm always the first to get picked on!"

"You know we love you, Chastity. That's why we pick on you so much!"

"Sure, it is!"

Joy looked at Hope. "Kolby wants me to take the day off work tomorrow. Is that a problem?"

"Of course not. I'll take your place at naptime."

"I think it's a good thing for you two to take a day after the wedding to just be alone. I think Hope and Faith should have done the same," Linda said.

Hope shrugged. "We had half a day off. It was fine."

Joy frowned at her sister for a moment. Something wasn't right with Hope's marriage. She wasn't sure what it was, but she was worried about her. "Kolby and I Skyped with Mom and Dad last night."

Hope's eyes widened. "What did they say?"

"Oh, you know Mom and Dad. They're not happy we're all marrying men they've not met. They want me to wait so they can come for the wedding. All that good stuff."

"Did you tell them I got married?" Hope asked, her face white. The fear they all had of displeasing their parents was obvious.

Joy nodded. "Yes, I did. They know we're in Wyoming, but not where."

"Did they ask about me?" Chastity asked.

Joy smiled. "Of course, they did."

"How furious are they?" Hope asked, her voice soft.

"About like you'd expect. Kolby didn't seem terribly impressed with them." Joy didn't talk about how torn she felt about the whole situation. She felt like she was caught between her sisters and her parents. She hated it.

"As long as they're not trying to find us, we're good," Hope said, turning away.

Joy nodded. "They're not." She knew she'd caused a bit of tension, although she'd never meant to. She didn't want to hide the fact that she was still in contact with their parents from the others, though. "Hope, can I borrow your car for a bit? I'd like to go for a drive."

Hope looked at Joy with surprise. "I guess that's all right. Are you going shopping?"

"No. Just for a drive." Joy took the keys Hope offered her. "Is it at Karlan's?"

"Yeah."

"Thanks. I'll be back before lunch." Joy left at that, not sure quite where she was going, but knowing she needed just a little time to think.

She made the short walk to Karlan's, not seeing anyone along the way. The men were all out on the range somewhere. The women were all working. She was glad. She needed some time to herself.

She got in the Equinox and started driving, not paying attention to the direction she was headed. She had the ranch's address in the GPS, so she wasn't worried about getting back.

Before she realized where she was, she found herself at the river Kolby had taken her to the previous week. She locked the car and got out. Walking along the path between the river and the mountains seemed the perfect way to get a grip on what she needed to do.

As she walked, she prayed about her situation. She was in love with the man she was going to marry, but he never planned to love her. Her parents were angry with her and her sisters for striking out on their own.

She thought about Marcus. She needed to text Grace and see if her sister would be willing to come out and meet the man. She wanted her there anyway. Grace was a wonderful baker and had been giving her baked goods away for a couple of years. Why, there hadn't been a wedding at their church without a Grace Quinlan cake in five years. And Grace was only twenty!

Faith went down the embankment to sit on the grass in front of the river, watching the ripples pass. She pulled out her phone and texted her sister, suggesting she and Honor join them in Wyoming. Within seconds, her phone rang.

Glancing at the screen, she saw it was Grace, and she wanted to clap with joy. It meant her sister was away from her parents and they could talk freely for a moment. "Gracie!"

"Joy! So good to hear your voice! Mom and Honor went grocery shopping, but I have a cold, so I asked to stay home. Do you really need us out there?" Grace was one to always get straight to the point.

"We do. There are some financial troubles with the ranch we're trying to work through."

"So what do you need me for?"

"There's no bakery in town. You could make a killing."

"I'll think on it. Talk to Honor. Are you married yet?"

Joy grinned, loving the way her sister got straight to the point. "Not yet, but I will be in about nine hours."

"Today? It's your wedding day?" Grace squealed. "I'm so excited for you, Joy! What does he look like?"

"I'll have one of the others text you pictures of the wedding. He's a tall, dark, and sexy cowboy."

"Sexy? I was sure you'd say tall dark and handsome."

"Oh, honey, handsome doesn't even begin to describe my Kolby. I take one look at him, and my insides turn to mush." She smiled dreamily across the water. "How are things at home without us there?"

Grace sighed heavily. "Mama's crying a lot. She's sad you're gone, but she's mad as well. She's keeping a closer watch on Honor and me."

"I'm sorry we're making things harder for you."

"Well, I don't blame you for it. I just...I'm ready to get out of here. Honor and I talked about calling your Dr. Lachele."

"Come out here. Please. You'd have so much more freedom."

"We're thinking about it."

Joy smiled, knowing she couldn't push her sister further than she had. "I have a man I want you to meet. His name is Marcus. He's a lawyer."

"A lawyer? Are you kidding me? Why would I want to meet a lawyer?"

Joy's eyes twinkled. "Well, you know how you've always loved telling lawyer jokes? Imagine dating a man who you could tell lawyer jokes to all the time!"

Grace laughed out loud. "Oh, that could be fun. Is he good looking?"

"Well, he's not a tall, dark and sexy cowboy, but he's attractive. He does wear a cowboy hat to church." Joy grinned. "You should see the pastor here. His name is Brother Anthony. He couldn't remember Hope's name during her wedding, and said, 'Do you insert bride's name here take this man?' I laughed so hard!"

"That is *hilarious*! He sounds cool. I'd tell you to have him Skype me, so we can 'meet,' but you know Mom."

"I do. We should have brought you with us."

Grace laughed. "Six women for the men to choose from instead of four? I don't think so."

"You have a point."

"Uh oh. Car door slammed. Gotta go. I hope your wedding is as beautiful as you deserve. I love you so much!"

"Love you too, Grace!" Joy realized her sister had cut off the call before her response, but she said it anyway.

She hugged her knees and watched the river, feeling it calming her. She was nervous about the wedding, but she was even more nervous about the wedding night. She had no idea what she was doing, and she hoped he wouldn't mind too terribly much. He sure didn't seem to.

She stayed there for an hour, fantasizing about the day when her husband would love her.

Finally, at just after eleven, she stood up and brushed off the seat of her jeans. She had grass all over her, but she didn't care. She walked back to the car and drove to the ranch, parking the vehicle at Karlan and Hope's house before walking back to the big house. As she was opening the back door, her pocket buzzed, and she pulled her phone out.

There was a text from Kolby asking her to have her things packed up and ready to move by noon when the men would be there for lunch. Joy rushed to her room. She could keep her make-up and a few other things there, but send everything else. Not that there was a whole lot to send. She was still waiting on most of her things to arrive from Kentucky.

She had everything setting on her bed in two suitcases and two boxes, keeping back her craft bag, the clothes she'd wear to the wedding, and her toiletries. Everything else could go.

Kolby found her in her room when he arrived. "You ready for this?" he asked softly, his eyes searching hers. He knew he'd hurt her feelings the night before, and he wanted to make sure she was all right.

Joy looked up into his brown eyes, stroking his cheek. "I'm very ready. Nervous, of course, but I think that's normal."

He dropped a kiss on her lips, pulling her close. "Are you nervous about the wedding or the wedding night?"

She blushed. "I've been to weddings before. I can handle that part of things."

"You'll handle the wedding night as well. I promise." He kissed her again, more slowly this time, his tongue moving in to tangle with hers. "Chris and I are going to move your things after lunch, so we don't have to mess with that after the wedding."

She smiled at that. "Sounds good to me. I spent the morning at your river."

He raised an eyebrow. "You did?"

"It calmed me so much. And I talked to one of my little sisters. I think they're going to come out and join the fight to save the ranch."

Kolby didn't comment on that. If she thought two more sisters and their crafts would help, he wasn't going to argue with her. "I'm glad it calmed you. Maybe we should have our wedding night out there."

She blushed. "I don't think so! We'll go to your house and have our wedding night in bed like normal people."

He leaned over and bit her earlobe softly. "We're going to make love by a river someday soon." Grabbing her hand he tugged her into the hallway and to the kitchen. "I'm starving."

The children had already been fed, and Hope was sitting with them, putting them all down for their naps. Joy and Kolby sank into their chairs at the table.

"I made grilled cheese and chips. The kids' new favorite."

Kolby smiled. "My favorite too, Mom. Well, other than ribs and layered dip of course."

Linda grinned at her son. "I made you layered dip for the reception, and an extra pan for you to take home with you. I know my boy."

"You really do love me!"

She laughed. "Of course I do. I love you enough that I'm even going to give Joy my recipe for layered dip."

Joy looked back and forth between mother and son. "How often do I need to make this layered dip?"

"Hourly," Kolby said quickly.

Linda looked at Joy. "Don't worry. I make it with a *Reader's Digest Condensed* recipe. It's easy!"

"I guess I'd better learn to make it then!"

"If it hair lips Georgia!" Linda responded.

"Who's Georgia?"

Kolby leaned over and whispered to Joy. "Just smile and nod. She says that all the time, and no one has any idea what it means!"

"Okay," Joy smiled sweetly at Linda.

"Did he tell you no one knows what that means?" Linda demanded.

Joy simply shrugged as Kolby squeezed her thigh under the table, silently thanking her for her silence. "I couldn't hear him very well," she fibbed.

After lunch, Kolby and Chris left to take Joy's things to Kolby's house while Joy worked on the castle she was making in the nap room. She had a hard time concentrating on the project, because all she could think about was how sweetly Kolby had made sure she was all right. He may not think he was in love, but he was kind, sweet, and gentle, always caring about her feelings. That made her very happy.

As soon as naptime was over, Joy sprang into action, rushing to get ready. She arranged her long red hair atop her head, leaving a few tendrils loose to curl around her face. Chastity knocked as she was putting the last of her craft things together to carry over to Kolby's after the wedding.

"Come in!"

Chastity bounced into the room, a gift in her hand. "I got you a wedding gift."

"When did you have time to shop for these things?" Joy asked. Chastity had gotten each of her sisters a gift as they married, but none of the others had taken the time out of their schedules to shop.

"Oh, I got them all before we left. There was this great little sex shop back home, and I used to sneak off to go there any chance I got. The owner knew me by name!"

"Of course, he did. I love you, Chastity, but you worry me."

Chastity shrugged. "Open it!"

Joy closed her eyes for a moment, praying it wasn't the same thing she'd given Hope. She did not need a vibrator that looked like it had been made for an elephant. Opening the box, she found a beautiful white satin teddy, covered in lace. It was much more tasteful than what Hope had received. "Oh, it's beautiful. Thank you!"

"I'm glad you like it!"

"I do!" Joy reached out and hugged her sister. "I'll wear it tonight."

Chastity hurried off then, leaving Joy to finish getting ready alone. She was surprised to admit it, but she missed her mom. Every time she'd pictured her wedding, her mother was by her side. She shook her head, realizing it wasn't possible, but wishing it was.

By the time for the wedding, she had worked herself up into a bundle of nervousness. Hope popped in to check on her, and Joy shook her head at her sister. "I can't do it. I can't marry him today."

Hope smiled, hurrying across the room. "What's going on, Joy? I've seen you look at him. I know you love him. Why don't you want to marry him?"

"I do want to *be married* to him. I just don't want to *marry* him. Can't you see the difference?"

Hope grabbed Joy's phone from her nightstand, immediately punching in a phone number and handing Joy the phone. "I'll give you some privacy." She left, closing the door behind her.

Joy looked at the phone and put it to her ear. "This is Dr. Lachele."

"Dr. Lachele, this is Joy Quinlan. I can't go through with it. I can't marry him."

"Sure you can. Okay, honeymuffin, sit your butt down, and let's chat."

Joy sat on the edge of her bed. "I'm sitting."

"What's going on? You're marrying Kolby, right?"

"Yes, ma'am."

"Why can't you marry him?"

Joy felt the tears start to fall, glad she'd worn waterproof mascara. "He says he's never going to love me!"

"He doesn't mean it, snookums. Kolby has been through a lot. I guess you know about the stupid underwear models and equally stupid women who are now married to them?"

Joy hiccupped a laugh. "Yes."

"Do you know about the girl he was about to propose to?"

"Rachelle? I didn't know he was about to propose, but I know he thought he was in love."

"Yeah, that idiot. Anyway, she messed with his head a little bit. Give him some time. Show him you're not like her. He'll come around. That man will be declaring his undying love within two weeks."

"Two weeks?" Joy laughed. "You think he's really going to love me within two weeks?"

"If not two weeks, then three. He'll love you soon. You have my word."

"You really think he's the one for me?"

Dr. Lachele sighed heavily. "I know he's the one for you. I'd have matched you two up. You were meant for each other. Now go marry the man and then take him to his house and do him like a wild woman!"

Joy shook her head. "My mother would be so appalled if she could hear you!"

"And that's why you called me and not your mother. Go on. When's the wedding?"

Joy looked at the alarm clock on the nightstand. "About five minutes ago."

"Get out there and see what Brother Anthony has to say this time. I have to say, I wish I could be in the congregation for every wedding that man officiates in. He's pretty awesome."

"Thank you, Dr. Lachele."

"You're welcome, sweet stuff. Be happy."

Joy put the phone down and got to her feet, looking down at her toes which were sticking out from under her dress. Seeing the pretty pink polish she'd put on them just hours before made her feel better.

She walked to the door and opened it, finding Faith waiting for her. "You ready?" Faith asked, her eyes seeming to understand what had happened.

Joy nodded. "I'm ready. I promised one of you would send pictures to Grace of the wedding."

Faith nodded. "I'll do it."

They linked arms and walked into the kitchen together, and then outside to where Brother Anthony was waiting nervously, plucking at his tie.

"Well, there's our bride!"

Joy leaned toward Faith. "Someone reminded him of my name, right?"

"I did, and so did Hope. I'm sure he's forgotten anyway."

Faith released her arm, walking to stand beside Cooper. Joy continued on alone, walking until she reached Kolby's side.

"Dearly beloved, we are gathered here today to help these two nice young people get hitched."

Joy heard Hope's laugh from behind her, and suddenly she felt free. This was going to be easy. Brother Anthony's ineptness at weddings made everything easier.

"Do you, pretty red-headed girl, take Kolby here to be your lawfully wedded husband? To love, honor, and kiss a lot 'til death do you part?"

Joy bit her lip to stifle the laughter, nodding. "I do."

"And do you, Kolby, take this pretty little thing to be your lawfully wedded wife? To love, honor, and have fun with for the rest of your life?"

Kolby looked deeply into Joy's green eyes. He nodded. "I sure do."

"Then you're married. Kiss her like you mean it, Kolby!"

Kolby pulled Joy to him and kissed her sweetly, his hands holding her a little closer than was really proper.

Joy had tears in her eyes when she turned to the people watching them. Her family.

# Chapter 7

During the short reception that followed, Kolby kept his eyes glued to his bride. His mother had baked a wedding cake which they cut together and fed to each other. When Joy's tongue touched his finger, it was all he could do not to pick her up and carry her off to his house right then. She was his wife now. There was nothing stopping him from making love to her, except all the people surrounding them.

After they'd had cake, Joy rested her head on his shoulder. "You know, Kolby, I was thinking."

He eyed her skeptically. "What were you thinking?"

"It's awfully peopley in here. Maybe we should go to your place where there are fewer people and more of just the two of us."

He grinned. "I have never heard anyone say anything smarter in my whole life." He grabbed her hand and dragged her over to his mother. "We're leaving. Remember, Joy's not working tomorrow."

Linda nodded. "I remember." She hugged Joy tightly. "Welcome to the family. I can't believe I already have three daughters!"

"Well, you'd better claim Chastity fast, because she's going to be the only one left, and she's ready for some individual attention."

Linda laughed. "I think I can handle Chastity."

Joy shrugged. "You've been warned!"

Kolby caught her hand again. "We're leaving," he called out over their chattering brothers and sisters, pulling her toward the door.

"Wait, we need to get the last of my things from my room."

He sighed. "Do you need them tonight?"

She started to say no, but then she remembered the teddy Chastity had bought her. "I do."

"Let's get them then." They walked to her room together, and he grabbed the two bags resting on the bed. "This it?"

She nodded. "If there's anything else, I can get it later in the week. That's all I need for tonight and tomorrow."

He kept her hand in his, not saying anything to the others as he dragged her toward the front door. He opened the passenger door on his truck and helped her in, noticing then her bare toes sticking out. "Did you get married with no shoes on?" he asked, obviously surprised.

"Real women don't wear shoes," she said calmly, tucking the full skirt of the dress around her.

Kolby shook his head as he threw her stuff in the back and walked around to the other side. He took her hand in his and brought it to his lips. "I'm so glad we're married."

She grinned at him, glad the actual ceremony was over. "Me too. And Brother Anthony didn't once refer to me as 'insert bride's name here.' I was amazed!"

"No, you were the pretty red-headed girl. I'm not sure why the congregation hasn't found another pastor, but he's been around for as long as I can remember." He drove quickly over the ranch's roads to his house, running around the truck to let her out again. "I still can't believe you were barefoot," he said as her toes stuck out from under the dress.

"Here's the real truth about me Kolby. I hate shoes. I would rather spend the rest of my life barefoot and never put on another high heel. I can deal with sneakers, but that's just about it."

"I guess I learn more about you every day." He helped her down and took her hand, leading her toward the house.

"I need the bags in the back," she reminded him.

He sighed. "You're not going to have any time for crafts tonight anyway."

She shrugged. "I still need my bags."

He walked to the back of the truck and got her things, carrying them into the house. "Happy now?"

She nodded. "Give me a minute. I'm going to go get ready for bed." Taking the bags from his hands, she walked into the bedroom and closed the door behind her.

Kolby stood looking at the closed door for a minute. Had she really just shut him out of his own bedroom?

He stalked back and forth across the living room, waiting for her to let him know she was ready. Finally, after what seemed like hours, he heard her call to him. "I'm ready!"

He hurriedly opened the bedroom door, and found her lying across the bed, her hair down around her bare shoulders. It was her attire that had his eyes popping out of his head. She wore a skimpy little white teddy. He swallowed hard. "Was that in the bags?"

She nodded. "A wedding gift from Chastity."

"She can buy you clothes any day." He kept his eyes on hers as he shrugged out of his suit jacket and draped it over the back of a chair. Then he removed his tie, and unbuttoned his shirt. "You look beautiful." He took off his socks and shoes, stalking over to her in just his slacks.

"Hi," she whispered softly, as he sat down on the bed in front of her.

"Hi." His hand reached out and he trailed one finger from the top of her shoulder down her arm. "You're so soft."

She sat up, moving both hands to his chest. "You're not."

He grinned. "I'm not supposed to be soft. You are." His lips brushed against hers. "Gizmo and I are very excited to reach this point in our relationship."

Joy's eyes sparkled with happiness. "Oh, really? Does Gizmo have some sort of special interest in me?"

He laughed. "He's dying to show you." He looked down at her scantily clad body, his eyes taking in every detail. "He likes that thing you're wearing."

"So kind of you to speak for him." She caught the back of his neck in her hands and pulled him to her for a kiss. "Share that with Gizmo, would you?"

"Oh, trust me. Giz felt that!" He stroked his hand over her bare arm, moving the spaghetti strap on her shoulder down. His lips quickly followed the path of his fingers. He knew he had to be gentle and take things slowly, but all he could think about was laying her down and spreading her thighs.

Joy stroked his chest, glad that she didn't have to feel guilty about touching him. She'd wanted this from the second day she'd known him, but she'd refused to hurry things along after she'd set the time frame. "You feel so *good*!"

He laughed softly. "You do too. I love this little thing you're wearing, but all I want to do is take it off you!"

She blushed. "I think you have every right to do that."

Moving his lips back to hers, he lowered the strap on her other arm and pooled the garment about her waist. Pulling back, he looked at what he'd uncovered, making his admiration of her obvious. "You're so beautiful."

Joy had never in her life truly felt beautiful until that moment, with him looking at her as if she was a goddess sent down from heaven just for his pleasure. "You make me feel like I'm something more than I've ever dreamed of being."

He was startled at her words, pulling back to sit on his heels for a moment, and studying her face. "Don't ever believe you're lacking, Joy. I wish I'd met you five years ago, because you would have knocked my socks off."

She giggled. "If we'd met when I was seventeen, I think my daddy would have had a right to get upset."

He shook his head at her. "Are you going to let me compliment you and tell you what an incredible woman you are, or are you going to spend the whole night arguing with me?"

"You can tell me I'm incredible all night long if you need to."

"I do need to! And I'm glad you're going to be good about it, because Gizmo is going to start screaming if I don't kiss you again."

She nodded, her face serious. "We must keep Gizmo happy."

He pushed her backward onto the bed, following down beside her. His lips moved back to hers, more demanding this time. His hands stroked over her breasts, pushing the teddy over her hips and down her legs. He tossed it to the floor, staring at her body for an instant. "Never wear clothes again."

She grinned. "The children's parents might have something to say about that."

"You have to argue with everything I say, but that's all right. I know the secret of keeping you quiet." His lips went back to hers, his hands stroking her urgently.

Joy lost herself in the kiss, happier than she'd dreamed she could be with him. He may not love her yet, but he was kind, gentle, and caring. She could be content with that for now.

As his hands stroked her, Joy found herself thinking less and less. One hand moved between her thighs, stroking her urgently.

She arched against his hand, wanting so much more from him. When one finger gently slipped inside her, she clutched at his shoulders. "That feels so good, Kolby!"

He worked his finger in and out of her, trying to be certain she was ready for him. Gizmo was screaming for release from his fabric prison. When she clenched around him, letting out a loud moan, he smiled, knowing it was his turn.

He moved off the bed, stripping off his slacks and rejoining her. This time he knelt between her spread thighs, waiting until she opened her eyes to look up at him. "You do bring me joy," he muttered before plunging inside her.

Joy gasped in pain, but lay still beneath him, waiting for him to begin moving inside her. When he didn't, she stroked his stomach. "What are you waiting for?" she asked.

He grinned. Only his Joy would react like that. "I was waiting for you to be ready." He leaned down to kiss her softly as he started moving within her.

Every movement he made had Joy writhing with pleasure. She gripped his shoulders tightly, trying to urge him on. "I can't believe how good this feels!"

He chuckled. "Gizmo is pleased you like him!" Moments later, he felt her clenching around him, and he knew he could let go. He crushed his lips to hers as he climaxed, shaking against her.

A short while later, he rolled to his side, gathering her close against him. "You're an incredible woman, Joy Culpepper. I'm going to keep you."

She smiled, her head pillowed on his chest. "There was a question before now?"

He grinned. "You trying to twist my words and get me in trouble?"

Looking him in the eye, she shook her head. "Of course not. For now, I'm happy to be here in your arms."

"Only for now?" Kolby felt his heart beating rapidly. Was she suggesting she was going to leave him?

"I can't promise I'll be happy tomorrow, but I know I'll never leave you. I believe in forever marriages."

He gathered her closer, kissing her forehead. "I do too. You scared me for a minute there."

Snuggling against him she sighed. "Good. Turnabout is fair play!"

He reached out, snapping off the lamp beside the bed. "Go to sleep, wife."

She closed her eyes and surprised herself by doing just that.

* * *

When Joy woke the next morning, Kolby was propped on one elbow, watching her sleep. She blinked twice to clear the fog from her eyes.

"G'morning," he whispered, kissing her softly.

"How long have you been awake?" she asked, glancing at the clock beside the bed. It was just after six.

"Thirty minutes or so."

"Just lying there watching me?"

"Well, yeah. You're beautiful, and you're my wife."

She blushed. "I'm glad I'm your wife." And in that moment, she was. She couldn't believe her good luck, to be married to a man as incredible as he was. "What do you want to do today?"

He raised an eyebrow, a grin spreading over his face. "I can't believe you even feel the need to ask me that."

Her blush deepened. "Do you want to go for a picnic later maybe?" Surely he didn't want to spend the *entire* day in bed!

"I'm not sure I want to leave the bedroom today."

"You have to eat, you know," she said with a stern frown.

"You're not going to offer me breakfast in bed? I'm wounded!"

She rolled her eyes. "I'll make you breakfast to eat at the table. How's that for a deal?"

He made a show of contemplating her question. "I guess I can settle for that. Better than the cereal I'd make for myself."

"I didn't say *what* I'd make you for breakfast. I think I'm going to adopt your mother's cooking strategies. The easier, the better."

He sighed heavily. "I was hoping for biscuits and gravy with eggs and sausage."

She rolled her eyes. "Well, I bought some Pillsbury biscuits at the store yesterday!"

"Sounds good to me. Is there any other kind?"

"Let me go get breakfast then."

He caught her by her waist before she could roll out of bed. "You don't want to kiss your husband good morning first?"

"We kissed."

Kolby frowned. "I kissed you. It's your turn to kiss me."

"Oh, is that how it works?"

"Yes. And I've initiated almost all of our kisses so you owe me a *lot* of them!"

"I had no idea I was falling down on the job so badly." Joy turned to him and kissed him, not noticing that the covers slid from her shoulders in the process. "Good morning."

"Mmm...g'morning." He kissed the tip of her nose. "Now, about wake up sex..."

She laughed. "Is that how we're supposed to start our mornings?"

"It's in the marriage rule book! Every single morning you kiss your husband, and then beg him to make love to you. Didn't you read the rule book?"

"I guess I must have missed that part." Joy looked Kolby straight in the eye. "Please, Kolby, will you make love to me? I couldn't face my day without you and Gizmo making it special for me!"

"Good wife," he whispered, leaning down to capture her lips with his.

* * *

An hour later, showered and dressed, Joy fixed the breakfast Kolby had requested. She'd expected to spend her life spoiling a man and her children, having grown up with 1950s values, so it didn't bother her to do it.

When Kolby came in from the shower, he took a deep sniff of the aroma of the sausage. "Now that's a breakfast."

Joy grinned. "You're going to expect to be spoiled rotten every day, aren't you?"

Kolby grinned, nodding slightly. "Of course, I am. My mom has been spoiling me all my life. Now it's your turn."

She sighed. "I always expected to spoil a man, but I hoped that he wouldn't be used to being spoiled so it would seem special to him."

He walked around behind her and wrapped his arms around her. "Anything you do for me is very special."

She leaned back against him. "I'm glad you think so."

After they'd finished breakfast, she turned to him, smiling. "I was so nervous yesterday, but I lived through the wedding *and* the wedding night. I'm happy it's all behind us."

He smiled, stroking her cheek. "Now we just get to enjoy our lives together."

"And live happily ever after?"

He shrugged. "As happily as anyone ever does." He watched her face fall a bit. "Do you want to go for a walk today? There are so many beautiful parts of Wyoming you've never seen. Or you could pack a picnic and we could just drive until we see a good place to stop and eat it."

Joy bit her lip, contemplating for a moment. She wanted to dwell on what he said and cry for a minute, but there was no point. She needed to be joyful after all. "Let's go for a drive. I'll pack a lunch."

"We could always stop for fast food as well, but it would be cheaper if we took something with us."

"And right now we're doing what we can to save every dime. So I'll pack a lunch." She quickly loaded the dishwasher while he brought her the picnic hamper he'd used the last time. She made sandwiches and put the covered pan of layered dip his mother had sent home with them in it before adding a bag of chips. A few more things went into the basket, and she was ready.

He carried the basket while she went and found her shoes. When she was ready, she followed him out to the truck. He was sitting in it listening to a country song. She got in beside him, reaching for his hand automatically. They had a one-day honeymoon, and she was going to be as close to him as she could.

He grinned at her. "I can't shift and hold your hand. Wait 'til we're on the highway, and it's all yours."

While they drove, they talked. There were so many basic things she didn't know about him. "Did you attend college?"

He shook his head. "I didn't. I knew what I was going to do and where I was going to be, so I didn't see the need."

"Do you ever regret that decision?"

He shook his head. "No, I really don't. I love what I do. I thought for a short while about going on the rodeo circuit, but I realized that wouldn't be nearly as fulfilling for me as doing the actual work on a ranch."

"I think you made a smart decision."

"What about you? Are you glad you went to college?"

"Oh, yes! We needed a way to get out of the house for several hours a day, and I feel like I learned some good skills to use in life."

"Well, that's good at least." He glanced over at her for a second before training his eyes back on the road. "Do you ever get angry at your parents for the way they raised you?" Between the things she'd told him, and the things he'd heard from his brothers, he knew her upbringing had been anything but jovial.

"Not really. I know they did what they thought was right. I don't think it's the way a child should be raised, but they believed it with everything inside them. I think not having any choices is way too restrictive, though. Do you realize I've never seen a movie that wasn't rated G? I've never watched network television. I was only allowed to watch shows like *Little House on the Prairie*, and then only on DVD, so I wouldn't accidentally change the channel. Don't get me wrong, I love *Little House*. But sometimes I think we should have been given some freedom to see what we would have chosen for ourselves."

"So you've never watched sitcoms or anything? Did you get to see Brady Bunch?"

She nodded. "We watched a few of the episodes, before Mom decided we should be doing something more constructive with our time. I don't think you understand the kind of control our parents exerted over us though. Our friends would all be going to see a movie, and none of us were allowed to go. We couldn't go to friends' birthday parties unless our parents had spoken at length about them. I never went to a school dance." Sighing, she shook her head. "I seriously feel like I've gone from living the life of a ten-year-old to the life of a grown adult in the space of a week. It's ridiculous."

"Well, we'll have to sit down and watch a few episodes of the raunchiest sitcom I can come up with. There's got to be something."

She laughed at that. "I don't need raunchy. I just don't need perfectly clean all the time."

"I can understand that. Do the twins feel the same way?"

"Honor and Grace feel very restricted in all they do. I texted Grace yesterday, and she was only able to call me back because Mom was grocery shopping and Dad was at work. I'm sure they consider the others and I bad influences on the twins now."

"That's sad."

"It is! I want them to come out here so badly. It's like there's suddenly a world that's opened up to me, because I left that place." She shrugged. "Someday Mom and Dad are going to come out here and visit, and they're not going to be happy. My mom would have a hissy fit if she saw the kind of stuff your mother uses to prepare meals."

Kolby didn't understand. "What does that mean? What does she do?" He'd never known anyone to prepare meals differently than his mother did.

"She uses short cuts. Pillsbury. Until last week, I had never made biscuits any way but from scratch. And she uses cake mixes."

"What's wrong with Pillsbury and cake mixes?"

"Mom doesn't think women should try to make their lives easier with short cuts. She thinks our sole purpose on earth is to take care of our men, and we shouldn't worry about how much work it takes. We should do it with a smile."

"You know that's just a little bit crazy, right?" He was driving through the mountains she'd enjoyed seeing in the distance, and was driving up a very steep road.

"Where are we going?"

He smiled at her. "Well, this road will get us most of the way up this mountain. I think we can get high enough to see some snow."

She grinned. "That sounds fun!"

They couldn't go all the way to the top of the mountain, but he took her to a small park that was high enough up to satisfy her curiosity. There was no one there. "In the summer, this place gets pretty full," he told her. "But all the kids are still in school, and it's still too cold for anyone to really want to spend time this high up in the mountains."

"Except us."

"Well, of course, except us." He brought her fingers to his lips. "Walk with me?"

She nodded. She'd expected they would do some walking. She slipped her feet back into her shoes. "I'm ready."

He watched her movement. "You really have a shoe problem!"

"If God had wanted me to wear shoes, I'd have been born with them on my feet!"

He laughed. "I had no idea you felt that strongly about it."

"Well, I didn't want you to refuse to marry me just because I had a shoe problem."

He leaned over and pressed a kiss to her lips. "I think I can handle your little shoe problem."

They got out of the truck and met at the front. He reached for her hand. "There's a walking trail over that way if I remember correctly."

She had to half-jog to keep up with him. "Kolby, your legs are a lot longer than mine!" she finally protested.

He slowed down. "Sorry about that. I forget sometimes."

She shrugged. "I'm not exactly tall, and you're huge!"

"Every man wants to hear that from his wife."

She blushed. "I wasn't talking about Gizmo."

"Trust me. You're always talking about Gizmo!"

She shook her head and followed him. The man was insane. No doubt about it.

# Chapter 8

For the next couple of weeks, Joy worked hard on her craft, and building up her online presence to be able to sell the things she made. She and Chastity often worked closely together, knowing they would be sharing an Etsy account and an eBay account.

Faith had a website for her baby doll business, and it was thriving. Her supplies had come in, and she spent a lot of time at her own home, doing the work she loved.

When she'd been married a little over two weeks, Joy and her sisters gathered in the master bathroom at the big house. They had all agreed with Joy's idea for them to take pregnancy tests together, and Joy's stomach was jumping with excitement. Her sisters all looked dreary and seemed to be going through the motions, but Joy was ecstatic at the prospect of being pregnant.

After she took the test with her sisters, and they'd lined them all up on the counter, Joy put her hand over her stomach and said a prayer. A baby was what she wanted more than anything. It wasn't simply part of the agreement she'd signed. Instead, it was something she wanted for herself and for Kolby.

She had in the back of her mind that as soon as Kolby found out she was carrying his child, he would fall to his knees and declare his love. She could see it in her mind. If she wasn't pregnant this month, surely she would be next. With the way they were going at each other, she didn't think it could possibly take more than a month or two.

She participated in the conversation her sisters were having, but she really wasn't there with them mentally. She was too busy counting down the minutes until the tests were ready. They had agreed to wait a full three minutes after the last test was taken before they looked. It was the longest three minutes of Joy's life. Of course, since she'd orchestrated the whole thing and tested first, she was waiting a bit longer than the others.

When it was finally time, she leaned over the tests. She had lined them up, so only she knew which was which. She didn't look at the others, only her own. Chastity's shout of, "Two! Two of them are positive!" came from afar. Because the one she was most worried about was positive. She stood straight up, stunned, her hand covering her stomach, wanting to touch the tiny life growing there.

She watched in shock as Faith ran from the room. Looking back at the tests, she realized Faith was the other positive. Didn't she want to be pregnant?

Hope walked over to Joy after Faith left. "Who are the two?"

"Faith and me. I'm so sorry you're not pregnant, Hope."

Hope shrugged. She seemed to truly not care, which surprised Joy. "Maybe next month. And only one of us needs to have a baby on the way. You and Faith gave Chastity and me some breathing room."

Joy smiled. "Well, I'll go sit with the kiddos and make some more furniture."

"Are you putting the castle up on eBay tonight?"

"I think I am. I'm so excited that it's finally time!" Joy headed back to the room where the children napped and sat down in her usual chair, picking up her craft tote. She wanted desperately to tell Linda, but she knew Kolby needed to know first.

As soon as she was done with her nap shift, she hurried home, deciding to make a special meal. She knew his favorite meal was steak, so she took some steaks out to defrost, and scrubbed some potatoes clean. She'd make him steak, potatoes, and a salad, and he would be a happy man.

She daydreamed about how it would be when she told him. Sitting down together at dinner, she would take his hand in hers. Then she'd quietly give him the news of their child. "We're having our first baby. Or babies. Whichever."

He would smile and stand up, pulling her to her feet so he could hold her close. "A baby! Marrying you has made my life complete. I love you, Joy. You've truly brought joy into my world."

He would sweep her into his arms and carry her to the bedroom, where they would make sweet love to one another, while he forgot all about his steak, because his passion for her would be all-consuming.

She sighed contentedly. She couldn't wait to tell him!

When Kolby got in from work, he was exhausted. "You look tired." It was all she could do not to blurt out her secret immediately.

He nodded. "It was a rough day. One of the heifers had trouble birthing her calf, so we had to call the vet. We can't afford to lose even two cows at this point. Our future lies in making sure they all stay alive through the summer." He yawned. "I'm going to bed right after supper."

Joy smiled, putting his plate on the table in front of him. She sat down beside him with her own plate, reaching for a sip of water. She started to tell him as soon as he took his first bite, but she decided she'd wait. He was obviously tired and hungry. She'd tell him when they were finished with their meal.

Once their meal was done, she went to wash the dishes while he showered. Joy still hadn't told him, but he could wait until after he was done in the bathroom.

She was waiting in bed for him when he left the shower. After he joined her, she snuggled close. "I have something to tell you."

"Are the twins coming?" He knew she'd been working with her sisters trying to get them to join them in Wyoming.

"No, not the twins." Her hand went to her belly. "I'm pregnant."

"That's nice." He yawned widely, not really taking in her words. "Wait? What? You're pregnant? Already?" He stared at her in shock. "We're having a baby?"

Joy nodded, her whole face lit up. She was glad he was responding the way he was. Now, he just needed to tell her he loved her. "Happened fast, didn't it?"

"Sure did. You just couldn't keep your hands off me." He shook his head at her, teasing laughter in his eyes. "I'm so happy!"

"Me too. I want this baby so much!"

"Now we'll be able to keep the ranch for sure. Your sisters don't even have to get pregnant if they don't want to." He yawned again, and it was so wide, he was certain his jaw had popped. Cradling her against him, he closed his eyes.

Joy watched him fall asleep, still waiting for the praise and the words of love. When they didn't happen, she sighed and closed her eyes. He was just too tired. He'd tell her in the morning.

* * *

Joy walked to the big house the following day dejectedly. Kolby hadn't told her he loved her. He'd said no words of love or praise. He'd simply gone to sleep. This morning, he'd asked if she was feeling sick, and she'd waited for the words, but again, they hadn't happened.

Why hadn't he told her? Maybe he was waiting for her to tell him first. That had to be it! She'd tell him at supper. Once he knew she loved him, surely he'd tell her. That was what he was waiting for.

True to her promise to herself, after supper that night, she sat with him while he watched a baseball game. She did some stitching on a new project, ignoring the television.

"I love you." She hadn't meant to blurt it out like that, but she couldn't help it. She needed the words, and obviously that was the only way she was going to get them.

Kolby looked over at her, a wariness entering his eyes. "You don't have to say that."

"But it's true."

"Thank you, then." He turned back to the television, his heart aching for her. He wasn't capable of love, and he hated that she seemed to think he was, despite his assurances that he wasn't.

Joy stared at him in shock. She poured her heart out, and he said, "Thank you?" What kind of man did that?

Jumping up from the couch, she ran into their bathroom, locking the door and starting the shower. If he couldn't come up with a better response than that, he didn't deserve her love!

Kolby stared at the TV, knowing he'd said the wrong thing, but how could he say the right thing? He wouldn't lie to her!

After her shower, Joy climbed into bed, wearing her oldest rattiest nightgown. She didn't want him to touch her ever again. As far as she was concerned, the marriage was over.

Kolby found her that way when he went to bed an hour later. She'd obviously cried herself to sleep, and he wanted to apologize and make everything right. But how could he? He didn't love her. There was no love left in him.

He watched her sleep for a minute before snapping off the light and closing his eyes. He had never hated himself quite as much as he did at that moment.

* * *

Joy got up the following morning and fixed Kolby's breakfast as if nothing had happened. When he came into the kitchen to get his food, he thanked her for cooking and she curtly said, "You're welcome."

He watched her as he ate, noting that she was obviously still angry. He pulled his phone from his pocket and texted Karlan. "Trouble at home. Going to be late."

As soon as she was finished eating, he caught her wrist and pulled her back to the bedroom. There was nothing in a new marriage that good sex couldn't fix, right? He pushed her onto the bed and pulled off his clothes, moving down to lie beside her.

"You're so beautiful," he whispered in her ear, knowing that hearing those words always made her happy.

When Joy didn't respond, he looked at her face. There was no expression. None of the happiness that was always there. Just a blank look and eyes that were filled with tears.

"Joy, talk to me."

"I don't believe there's anything left to say. I said everything that I needed to say last night. And you said, 'Thank you.' It's my job as your wife to have sex with you when you need it, but don't expect me to enjoy it."

He gaped at her. "What do you mean?"

"I mean, that I'll do my duty as your wife, because I was raised to be a good wife. I will not be happy about it though."

Kolby rolled off the bed and gathered his clothes, dressing quickly. "I would never force myself on you, Joy."

"It's not force if I agree."

He closed his eyes. "I didn't mean to hurt you."

Joy closed her eyes, waiting until she heard his footsteps leave the room. She didn't even want to look at him.

When she heard the front door slam, Joy reached for her phone, punching in the number for Dr. Lachele.

"Hey there, Joy. What's going on in your world?"

Joy let out a little sob in response. "You said he'd come around and fall in love with me. I told him I was pregnant, and he was happy about the baby, but he didn't tell me he loved me. I figured he was waiting for me to say it first, so I said it last night. Do you want to know what he said?"

There was a moment of silence on the other end of the phone. "What did he say?"

"He said, 'Thank you.' I poured my heart out, and told him exactly how I feel about him, and he thanked me!"

"Give him a little more time."

"I've given him weeks. I've been a good wife. I cook for him. I clean for him. I'm always willing in bed. I'm carrying his child! And he thanked me. Sometimes the only purpose a man serves is target practice!"

"Sometimes that's true. Here's the deal though, Joy. You now have to go about your day, but you don't have to do it with a smile on your face. You have every right to be angry, so you should be. You should shout. You should cry. Throw things at him if you need to!"

"But I'm *Joy*!" How could she possibly unleash the emotions Dr. Lachele was talking about? It was her job to remain joyful for those around her.

"I don't want you to go to the daycare today," Dr. Lachele said after a minute. "Borrow a car and go down to the water. You know how that calms you. You'll see things more clearly when you get back."

"Lot of good that's going to do!" Joy yelled at the older woman.

It was a good thing she couldn't see Dr. Lachele's face, because the older woman was smiling.

* * *

Joy followed orders and texted Hope, telling her she not only wouldn't be there, but she wanted to borrow her car. When she walked to the big house, Hope was playing with the children. Joy walked to her and held her hand out. "Keys."

Hope dug for the keys in her pocket. "Are you all right, Joy?"

Joy looked at her sister, all of her anger piling up. "No, I'm not all right, but do you know what? That's fine! I don't always have to run around with a smile on my face. I'm allowed to not be happy. Did you know that? Did you know it's not my job to keep everyone around me joyful?" She hissed the words at Hope, not wanting the children to hear. "And when you fight with the others from now on, I'm going to just let you do it. I don't need to always jump in the middle and fix everything. It's not my job!"

Hope stood staring after her sister as she strode off. The look of shock on her face would have made Joy laugh, if she had seen it.

Joy walked to Karlan and Hope's house, getting behind the wheel of the Equinox. She knew she could take Kolby's truck, but the louse had never bothered to teach her to drive a stick shift. Her dad had claimed girls were incapable of learning, but she didn't believe that nonsense for a second.

She drove down to the river, climbing down the embankment to sit on the edge. All around her were flowers and the beauty of spring, and all she wanted to do was hit someone. She'd never hit anyone in her life, but she knew it would be gratifying.

As she sat, she cried. She dug up some of the grass on the bank of the river and threw it into the river. She wanted to kick and scream, but she kept it all inside.

She had no idea how long she was there. She had shut off all sound on her phone, refusing to deal with anyone. Why did she care if anyone worried about her? All they wanted from her was a vapid smile anyway. No one cared what was really going on in Joy Culpepper's mind. Why would they?

* * *

Kolby went to his mom's for lunch as usual. Most days Joy was already in the back with the babies, but he wanted to sit with her for a minute, and talk to her calmly. He knew she wouldn't yell in front of the children.

"I'm going to take my lunch back and eat with Joy," he announced.

Linda gave him a level look. "Joy didn't come to work today."

"She didn't? Why not?"

"She's mad about something," Hope said. "She wouldn't tell me what, but she's furious. I've never in my life seen Joy angry before today."

"You've never seen your sister angry? Don't you think that's odd?" Kolby asked.

"I don't care if it's odd or not. You made her angry, and now you need to fix it."

Kolby sighed. "Do you know where she is?"

Hope shook her head. "She borrowed my car, and she took off in a huff. You need to go find her."

"Are you sure? I think I know where she is, but maybe she needs to be alone for a while? So she can get over her anger."

"I don't know if she even knows how to get over anger. Since we were little, Mom told Joy that it was her job to always be joyous. And Joy believed her. Any time she felt any negative emotion, she'd just plaster a smile on her face and keep going. She's not doing that this time, which is good, but I don't know what you'd find if you went after her!"

Linda spoke up at that point. "Lachele was worried about her so she called me so someone could keep an eye on her. Lachele told me that Joy thinks the only thing you're good for is target practice. If you go, take something soft she can throw at you. Might help."

Kolby stared at his mother in disbelief. "You want me to give her ammunition against me?"

"Take marshmallows. I think eggs or tomatoes would make her feel better, because they're better projectiles, but take something. You made her mad, so you get to make her happy."

"You don't even know what happened! Why are you taking her side against mine?"

"Because I know both of you. You could make a preacher take up drinking."

He rolled his eyes. "Do you really think I need to take her something to throw at me?"

Linda nodded. "Stop at the store and get some tomatoes. She's worth it."

Kolby sighed, walking home quickly. He grabbed a towel and a few bottles of water, before making her a sandwich in case she hadn't had lunch.

# Chapter 9

Stopping at the grocery store in town, he drove to the river, knowing that's where she'd be.

He spotted Hope's car immediately and knew he was in the right place. He shoved everything into a backpack, and walked the trail, trying to find his missing wife.

Finally, he spotted her, in almost the exact same spot where he'd asked her to marry him. He walked down the embankment, sitting beside her. "I was worried you hadn't eaten." He pulled out the sandwich he'd made, a bag of chips, and a bottle of water.

"I'm not hungry."

"You have to eat. You're carrying a baby."

She glared at him, taking the food from him and forcing a few bites down. It tasted like sawdust.

"I'm sorry I've hurt you. I never meant to." She kept her face turned away from him, so he continued. "Mom said you wanted to use me for target practice."

"Are you volunteering?" she asked, knowing Dr. Lachele must have said something to his mother. At first she was furious, and then she realized that the matchmaker had probably done it so Joy wouldn't hurt herself.

He nodded. "I brought tomatoes."

Joy blinked at him. "Are you serious? You'll go be my target and let me throw tomatoes at you?"

"I will. I don't ever want to hurt you. I know I have. I can let you throw tomatoes at me if it will make it so you can smile again."

Joy contemplated for a moment. It wasn't what she needed most, but it probably would make her feel better. "Are they rotten tomatoes?"

He made a face. "No, I just bought them at the grocery store in town. They're ripe tomatoes." He hoped she wouldn't take him up on it, but he'd let her if she needed to.

"Give them to me."

He pulled the package of tomatoes out of the bag and handed them to her. "Where do you want me?" he asked.

She pointed to a tree about ten feet away. "Stand in front of that."

Kolby took a deep breath, wanting to refuse, but he'd offered. He knew his Joy wouldn't really hit him with the things anyway. He walked over and stood in front of the tree.

Joy peeled the cellophane off the package, and took the first tomato in her hand. It wasn't quite mushy enough to suit her tastes, but she didn't care at that moment. She threw it overhand, aiming for his face.

When she hit her target, she put her hand over her mouth in shock as he used the back of his hand to wipe the juice off his face. "Feel better?"

"A little." She surprised even herself when she reached for the next one. And the next.

When Joy ran out of "ammunition," she started looking around for something else to throw. Her sandwich was next, flying apart as it sailed toward him through the air. "You should have bought more tomatoes!"

Kolby stalked toward her, reaching down and opening the backpack. He removed the towel and the clean shirt he'd packed, wiping his face clean. "Feel better now?"

She folded her arms across her chest. "Only a little."

"Can we talk now?" he asked, shrugging out of the shirt he was wearing and slipping the T-shirt over his head.

"Why? My feelings don't matter to you at all!"

He frowned. "They matter to me a great deal. That's why we had our talk about me never loving again before we married. Remember that talk?"

She turned her back on him, refusing to listen.

"Joy, I care about you a great deal. And not just because of the baby you're carrying. I never wanted to hurt you."

She spun around to glare at him. "Well, you did! When a girl says I love you, even if you can't say it back, you don't thank her! 'I care for you.' 'You're important to me!' Either one of those would have been so much better!"

"You're right. They would have. I froze and didn't know what to say or do. But do you want to know *why* I froze?" he asked. "Because I care about you so much. You're an incredible woman, and a better wife than I deserve."

She studied him for a minute, trying to make sense of his words. "So you acted like a jerk because you care, not because you don't?"

"Well, I think the word 'ass' describes how I acted better than jerk, but yeah. That's the bottom line."

Joy frowned. "I've never had a temper tantrum in my life. I sat here thinking about hitting you. I honestly pictured myself balling up my fist and punching you in the face."

"At least you weren't out for Gizmo," he said sadly, shaking his head.

She shook her head. "Gizmo is not the head causing my problems." She noticed tomato seeds in his hair and did her best not to giggle. He looked ridiculous.

He took her hands in his, taking it as a good sign when she didn't immediately pull away from him. "I'm very sorry for any pain or heartache I've caused you. You mean so much to me."

She sighed. "I guess my little fit was over the top."

Kolby shook his head. "No, I think it was just what you needed. You are a warm, loving, passionate woman. With passion comes anger as well. You need to be able to show your anger."

She shook her head. "No, I need to be joyful. It's my name after all."

Kolby leaned down until they were nose to nose. "No, you don't. You need to be able to feel emotions and express them. You have to be able to live and be who you are, no matter what kind of crap your parents have been telling you for the past twenty-two years!"

Joy stared into his eyes for a minute. "You didn't mind?"

"Well, I didn't like having tomatoes thrown at me very much, but I agree I deserved them. I didn't mind you getting angry. I'd rather you didn't get angry with me every day, of course, but occasionally I'm sure I'll deserve it."

Joy caught him around the neck and pulled him down the last inch for a kiss. "You've just given me the greatest gift I've ever received." Her voice was a whisper, but it was filled with emotion.

Kolby caught her around the waist and pulled her closer to him. "I'd have told you that the day we met if I'd realized you were afraid to show any emotions." His hand stroked over her back. "You know the park is dead today. We could make love by the—"

"It's not happening!" she interrupted, her face in flames. "No way."

"We're not making love, or we're not making love by the river?"

She smiled. "Let's go home."

He grabbed her hand and tugged her along after him. "We'll both drive to Karlan's house, and you can get in my truck from there. I'll drive you the rest of the way home. We'll get to bed faster that way."

Joy shook her head. "Letting Gizmo take over again?"

He nodded. "I think you prefer it."

"Sometimes!"

When they reached the vehicles, he kissed her softly. "I'll see you at Karlan's."

As she drove, Joy thought about the freedom her husband had just given her. He'd said he cared about her, and she was allowed to show any emotion she wanted. For years, she'd felt like she had to be a happy robot outwardly, unable to be who she really was. Now, with his permission, she would show whatever emotion she really felt. Look out world!

* * *

Joy put her newfound freedom to use that very evening. Kolby was sitting in front of the television watching a ball game, and she was trying to talk. When he didn't listen, she reached over for the remote in his hand, and snapped the TV off.

He turned to her, glaring. "Why did you do that?"

"Because you were ignoring me, and I was tired of it. You want to see my emotions, well, this is how I feel about it. When you ignore me, it makes me angry."

He turned to her. "What were you saying?"

"I was trying to talk about potential names for the baby. Remember her? The little thing growing inside me?"

"Her? How do you know it's a girl?"

"I don't. I'm calling it her until there's reason to do otherwise."

"I see. Do you have names picked out?" He wanted to make sure she didn't get mad enough to throw tomatoes again, even though he thought it was much too early to discuss names.

"Not yet. Do you have any naming conventions you want to use? Or do you just want to randomly pick names we like?"

"What do you mean by naming conventions?"

"Well, like my sisters and I all having positive character traits as names. And you and your brothers all having the 'k' sound, even though you don't all have the same first letter to your name."

Kolby shrugged. "I guess I've never really thought about it. Do you want to do that?"

"I don't know. I once thought I did, but I'm really not sure. I could go either way."

"Do you have any names in mind?"

"Not yet. I want us both to be thinking about it." She reached for his hand. "I need to get medical attention soon. Would you be willing to have a home birth? With a midwife?"

He laughed, assuming she was joking. When he realized she wasn't, his eyes widened. "Really?"

"Really. I've always thought that's the route I'd go."

"Is that safe for you?" He wouldn't risk her for anything.

"Women had babies at home for thousands of years. It's only in the last century that they started having babies in hospitals."

"But hasn't the death rate from child birth dropped significantly during that time? I'm not going to risk your life for any reason."

Joy smiled, her eyes lighting up. His words, even though they weren't the declaration of love she so desperately wanted, would keep her going for a while. "If there's any risk, the midwife would transfer me to the care of an obstetrician. I won't do anything to risk our baby."

"Or you?"

She snuggled against him. "Or me." Her eyes twinkled as they met his. "I can only imagine how you'd handle a baby on your own. I can't be out of the picture."

He grinned at her teasing. "No, you can't. I need you beside me, Joy." His lips were soft against hers. He abruptly got to his feet and scooped her into his arms.

"Where are we going?"

"Where do you think?"

She shook her head. "I can't ever just have a discussion with you..."

* * *

When Joy got to the big house the following day, she noticed how happy Hope looked. Linda was glowing, excited at the idea of her impending role as grandmother.

Joy joined her mother-in-law in the kitchen, helping fix the plates of the children. "You look happy!"

Linda nodded. "I am! I'm sure you know Faith is pregnant. I'm going to be a Wiggie!"

"I did know Faith is pregnant." Joy eyed Linda. Had no one told her she was having two grandbabies? "Did you know I'm expecting as well?"

Linda stared at her for a moment, grabbing her and hugging her. "No! No one told me!"

Joy grinned. "I thought you knew, or I'd have told you."

"Just don't have the babies on the same day. That would mess with my head."

"Yeah, and we come from a family where multiples are the norm. Imagine if we each had twins..."

"Don't get my hopes up!" Linda finished putting the last of the food on paper plates, and Joy helped her serve the children.

Once the little ones were eating, Linda asked, "Are you doing better today?"

Joy shrugged. "A bit less angry. I've never been so mad in my life."

"Did you enjoy throwing the tomatoes at Kolby?"

Joy blushed. "You know about that?"

"It was my idea. I hope it helped."

"It helped a lot. I was so furious with that man!"

Linda shrugged. "When I had him, he was perfect. You must have done something to him."

Joy refused to comment. She loved her mother-in-law too much to cause problems, and just then she would have liked to strangle her. She knew Linda had to be loyal to her son, but claiming he was perfect? That went much too far!

# Chapter 10

Four weeks later, Joy felt like Kolby would never love her. He was kind, caring, and very considerate of her feelings, but love didn't seem to have any part of it.

One Sunday afternoon, after the men had finished work for the day, he came home. "Karlan needs me to run to town to pick up some stuff. Do you want to come with me?"

Joy shook her head. "No, my all-day morning sickness doesn't want to be anywhere near a truck." She patted her stomach lightly. "I think I'll sit around doing my stitching. If I don't move too much, there's less chance of me vomiting everywhere."

Kolby walked to her and hugged her tight. "Cooper said Faith is going through the same thing. Are you going to be all right?"

"Yeah, this is perfectly normal until the second trimester. Mom said with the twins, she threw up all nine months."

"Well, let's hope that doesn't happen." He hated seeing her so sick. She'd lost weight everywhere but her stomach, and that was starting to round a little. "Do you want me to stay? I'm sure Karlan or Chris can go. They don't have sick wives."

Joy smiled, resting her head on his shoulder. "I'm not an invalid. I can take care of myself."

"Then I'll go." He kissed the tip of her nose. "Why don't I grab a rotisserie chicken and some sides from the grocery store, so you don't have to cook?"

"Oh, that would be fabulous, if you don't mind."

"I'll be back soon." Hugging her once more, he headed for the door, worried about how frail she was looking. She'd been slender when they'd married, but the baby seemed to be leaching everything she could keep down.

In town, he parked in front of the hardware store, glancing at an older couple walking down the street holding hands. He'd gone to school with their grandsons. As he watched them, he could see him walking down the street in fifty years or so, holding Joy's hand the way old Mr. Larson was holding his wife's.

He frowned. He'd never let himself think about growing old with her, because he'd worried she'd leave.

As he bought the supplies he'd been sent to town for, he couldn't get the image of the older couple off his mind. He could picture Joy at that age, still as beautiful as ever.

He sighed. He needed to get her out of his head.

Next he went to the grocery store, finding the chicken and a couple of sides from the deli to go with it. He didn't want Joy to have to fight her morning sickness to cook for him. He laughed as he thought about the words everyone used for being sick with a baby. Joy was sick every hour of the day and night. Morning sickness didn't begin to cover it.

He realized once he got to the front that he was in Abigail's line. He didn't want to talk to her, but he didn't want to make a show of moving to another line either.

"Hey, Kolby! How's married life treating you?" she asked when it was his turn.

"Oh, good. Joy is a really special lady."

"I hear she's already expecting!"

Kolby grinned, the smile lighting up his whole face. "Oh, she is. I just wish we could keep something in her stomach. She's sick all day every day."

"Have you tried ginger tea? Or even ginger snaps? I find they really soothed my stomach when I was pregnant."

"Really? I'll go back and grab some."

Abigail shook her head. "No need. I'll send someone for them." She picked up her phone and requested the two items, and they stood there in silence for a moment. "I'm glad you found someone you could love, Kolby."

Kolby smiled. He wasn't about to tell Rachelle's sister that he wasn't in love with his wife. It was none of her business.

When a young man Kolby didn't know rushed to the front with his stuff, he paid and left the store, thinking about what Abigail had said. He saw the older couple again, this time heading into the store, and he wanted to stop them and ask them how they'd stayed together so long.

On the drive home, he was still thinking. He kept saying he couldn't love again, but what else was he feeling? Every time Joy threw up, he wished he could take her place. Every time she hugged him, he felt like his heart was flying. If that wasn't love, what was it?

He was so lost in thought that he almost didn't notice as a big truck crossed the center of the road, heading straight for him. At the last second, he turned the wheel, heading down into a ditch and toward a field. He ended up plowing his truck into a fence post before he came to a stop.

The whole time he was clutching the wheel with everything he had, he was thinking about Joy. *What if I die, and she never knows how I feel? What if our baby grows up without a father, and Joy can't tell him how much I loved them both?*

He got out and looked at his truck. There was some damage, but it was drivable. He got back in and headed toward home, knowing he had to say the words his Joy had been waiting to hear.

Kolby pulled up to the house, carrying the food he'd purchased in. He'd leave the hardware in the truck, because there was no reason to carry it in, when he'd just have to take it to work the next day.

As soon as he opened the door, he heard the familiar sound of Joy retching. After setting the food down, he went to the bathroom, to find her kneeling beside the toilet. Immediately he wet a wash cloth with cool water, and knelt beside her, wiping her face. "Are you all right, sweetheart?"

Joy looked at him for a moment, looking like she wanted to say something, before she turned back to throw up one last time.

He held her hair while she vomited, and whispered softly, "I love you, Joy."

Joy glared at him. "Did you really just tell me you love me for the first time while I was *puking*?"

Kolby shrugged. "I've never been known to have the best timing." He stroked her hair away from her face. "I realized it today. I can't imagine what my life would be like without you. I need you, Joy."

Joy sighed, resting her head against his shoulder. "Well, I'd love to continue this talk anywhere but the bathroom floor."

He got to his feet and carefully helped her up, watching while she brushed her teeth. "I got you some ginger tea and ginger snaps. Someone told me they'd soothe your belly."

"I'll try anything." She rinsed her mouth and looked at him, wondering why he suddenly felt like he could love again, when he'd been so adamant it wasn't possible.

He took her arm and led her out to the couch, sinking down beside her. "I'm sorry you're so sick. How about I bring you some ginger snaps? Or I can make you some tea?"

Kolby had been very attentive to her every time she'd been sick. Usually he just stood around, looking like he wished he knew what to do. Obviously he was pleased that he finally had an answer.

"Let's try the tea first. It's easier to throw up liquids." She watched him walk to the kitchen and filled the teapot with water, putting it on a burner. "Thank you for thinking of me."

He smiled. "I rarely think of anything else. All day while I'm working, I think of you."

"Do you really?" she asked. After so much time with him insisting he'd never love again, it was hard to believe.

"Of course, I do. I'd never lie to you, Joy." He carefully poured the hot water into the mug with the tea bag in it and added a spoon. Walking back around to sit beside her, he wrapped an arm around her waist. "I hope that helps."

Joy took a tiny sip of the amber colored liquid and set the mug down, not daring to drink too much at once. "What happened while you were gone?" she asked softly, knowing there had to be some catalyst to his abrupt change of heart.

He shrugged. "I saw an old couple in town, and all I could think about was growing old with you. And then I got into a kerfuffle with a fence post on my way home." At her look of alarm, he held up one hand. "Don't worry. I'm all right. Truck has seen better days, but we'll get it fixed."

Her eyes widened. "Are you sure you're all right?" She skimmed him from head to toe, looking for visible injuries.

"I'm fine! All I could think about as I was swerving off the road to miss that semi was you. I was so worried that I'd die without ever telling you how I feel." His hand reached out to stroke her cheek. "I love you so much."

Joy sighed contentedly, leaning against him. "I love you too. Thank you for loving me."

He chuckled.

"What?"

"Well, when you told me you loved me and I thanked you, you got all mad at me. Now I tell you I love you, and you thank me, but I'm not mad."

She glared. "You already knew I loved you when you said it to me. The situation is totally different."

He nodded. "It is. I'm so sorry I've hurt you."

Joy moved closer to him, snuggling against him. "I'm just glad you've finally had an epiphany and seen what an incredible wife you have."

"I have. I'll never take you for granted again."

"I sure hope not." She took another sip of the tea. "I think this may actually be helping."

"Good! I'm going to really worry about you if you lose any more weight."

"I'll do my best not to." She looked at him over the rim of the mug. "I think I've changed my mind about having fifteen kids. Maybe we could adopt fourteen or so."

He grinned at her. "I don't blame you. When is your first midwife appointment?"

"Tuesday. She's going to do a sonogram. Do you want to come with me?"

"I'd love that! Is Faith going too?"

She nodded. "I'm sure Cooper will be there as well. It'll be nice to see if we're having just one baby or two."

"Just not four, okay?"

Smiling, she nodded. "I'm in complete agreement with that. Anything more than two is too many."

"Mom wants as many as possible as soon as possible. She's so excited about being a Wiggie."

"She'll make a great Wiggie." She lifted a hand to his cheek. "But you'll make a great father."

He sighed. "I sure hope so. I want to be the best dad I can be to that little munchkin."

"There's no doubt in my mind you will be."

"What's the news on getting your sisters out here? Marcus has been bugging me about the date you promised him with Grace."

"Did he look over the will?" she asked, holding her breath for the answer.

He nodded. "He said it looks airtight. We need to keep doing what we're doing to buy Travis out, whether we like it or not."

"The girls need to come then. I'm sure they'll be here soon." She'd talked to her sisters just a few days before, and they were still undecided.

"I'm surprised they're not already here!" He couldn't imagine anyone choosing to stay with her parents.

"The four of us moving out has been hard on Mom. They're just trying to do what's right."

Kolby nodded, wishing they'd come sooner rather than later. "Are you feeling better? Do you want me to get you some food?"

"You don't have to take care of me, you know."

He smiled. "I know. But I want to." He leaned forward and kissed her softly. "Love makes you want to do some crazy things."

She laughed. "I don't know that I'd call taking care of me crazy."

"Maybe not." He smiled. "You've changed my entire life. I'm so glad Dr. Lachele sent you to me."

She smiled, basking in his love. She was married to a man she loved, carrying his baby, and now he loved her in return. What more could a woman ask for in life?

To receive notification of new books by Kirsten Obourne, click here.[1]

Chastity is going to be interesting to read about, isn't she? Check out an excerpt from her book, *Teacher's Troublemaker* by Merry Farmer coming April 8th, 2016.

---

1. http://eepurl.com/y6WRb

# Excerpt from Teacher's Troublemaker

Chastity Quinlan was a virgin. Still.

"Ugh," she snorted as she sat at one end of a comfy couch in Linda Culpepper's living room, knitting needles clicking away. "I once heard this phrase while watching a British movie: gagging for a shag." Her needles paused and she whipped to face Joy, who sat at the other end of the couch, poring through a catalog of supplies for her Barbie furniture venture. "Joy. I'm gagging for a shag. Totally gagging for it."

"Eew. That's gross." Faith wrinkled her nose from where she sat across the room, snuggled in Cooper's big, hot, masculine embrace as they watched TV.

Chastity stuck her tongue out at her sister. "Easy for you to say. You're getting it several times a day, if what I hear is right."

Faith tensed, her eyes going round with a 'You *heard* that?' sort of look.

"What?" Cooper blinked away from the baseball game that had him so transfixed, looking around as if he's missed something.

Ha! Cooper wasn't missing anything. Neither were Karlan or Kolby, Hope and Joy's husbands, if everything that normally went on in a marriage was going on with them. They too were absorbed in the baseball game, yapping on about stats and players and stuff that Chastity didn't give a fig about.

She scowled and focused on her knitting, needles flying as she knit a thin tube that would be a baby sock for one of Faith's dolls. It wasn't that she resented her sisters for their ability to get laid at a moment's notice if they so chose. She wasn't even mad at Chris, the youngest Culpepper brother, who she'd been flirting with for the past two weeks—like a homecoming queen with the captain of the football team at prom. She and Chris had an understanding, and they *needed* to get married to fulfill the terms of the Culpepper will. But she was so horny, what with all the sexual tension from her three newly-married sisters in the room, that she was going to need to sit on a towel if she wasn't careful.

"Where is Chris anyhow?" Linda asked as she walked into the room with a platter of sandwiches. The moment she put them on the table, baseball became the second most important thing in the room as Karlan, Cooper, and Kolby leapt from their chairs to load up on lunch.

"You want turkey or roast beef, sweetie?" Cooper asked Faith over his shoulder.

Faith was more interested in staring at Cooper's assets as he bent over the plate than answering. She finally managed, "Hmm? What? Huh? Oh, turkey."

Cooper noticed where her eyes had landed. He grinned. He winked. He wiggled his backside. Then he popped a turkey sandwich on a plate for her, carried it back to the chair, squeezed into it with her, and planted a big, wet one on her mouth.

"Gah." Chastity squirmed in her seat, pouring all her energy into knitting. She'd read her fair share of sexy romance novels. Maybe more than her fair share. She couldn't help but visualize gigantic, hard-bodied males slipping and sliding on top of—and under, and beside, and around—soft, nubile, female ones. As long as she fuzzed out the faces so that she wasn't gawping at her sisters and brothers-in-law in her sexed-up imagination, she'd be good. But, dangit, if she didn't get a little of that deep-tongue, hard-body action from Chris soon, she might go insane.

"Good Lord, Chastity, what on earth are you making?"

Linda's snappy question and the laugh that followed yanked Chastity out of her thoughts. She glanced down at the baby sock.

Only, it didn't look much like a baby sock anymore. It's started out that way, but after rows and rows of frantic, heated, energy-expending knitting, what she had in her hands was an eight-inch tube with a rounded end, flopping down from her fisted hands.

"Oh my gosh, Chastity, did you just knit a penis?" Hope laughed as she picked up a roast beef sandwich from the plate on the coffee table.

Chastity's mouth dropped open. "Holy crap! I've just had the best idea ever."

"Good grief," Joy muttered, sending Kolby a knowing look as he handed her a plate with a sandwich. "Don't tell me it's a penis idea."

"Johnson jammies!" Chastity held up her knitted tube. "Perfect for keeping the little guy warm and cozy on a cold winter's night."

Her announcement was met by uncomfortable silence and awkward glances from the guys. Faith winced, Hope choked and looked away, and Joy just shook her head.

"Uh, I don't think keeping it warm is a problem," Karlan muttered.

"Yeah," Kolby added slowly. "And you might want to make an opening at the end in case of, uh, nighttime emergencies."

Cooper snorted and choked around a bite of sandwich.

"Easy to do." Chastity turned her knitting around, studying it from different angles. "Very easy to do."

To do. As in doing. As in being done.

Damn, she wanted Chris to do her bad right then.

"Where is Chris anyhow?" she burst out.

"I'm in here." Chris's muffled voice came from the laundry room at the end of the hall.

Thank the good Lord above!

Chastity scooted forward, stuffing her little knitting project in the big, dorky bag where she kept her yarn, and launched herself off the couch. It was time she grabbed this whole marriage thing by the balls and—

"Hi Chris," she murmured in her best sexy siren voice as she slipped into the laundry room. She stretched against the doorframe, raising one arm and sticking out her hip, like an old photo of Marilyn Monroe she'd once seen.

"Hi Chastity," Chris replied, deep and throaty, totally in the spirit of seduction. His eyes smoldered, his lips twitched, and his jeans tented.

"What'cha doin'?" Chastity batted her eyelashes, directing her gaze to Chris's pants, wondering whether she would actually be able to see things swell.

Chris ran his tongue along his lip, shifted his hips just so, and lifted a handful of grungy white cotton. "I'm washing my dirty underwear," he answered as if describing how it got that way. "Seems I've been going through a lot of it lately."

"That is utterly disgusting," Kolby called from the living room.

"Yeah, some of us are trying to eat here," Cooper added.

In unison, Chris and Chastity broke down into silly laughter. Their ridiculous characters and goofy mood was broken. Chris winked at her, then turned to finish loading his whites into the washing machine. Chastity shut the laundry room door, then crossed to lean her backside against the dryer.

"Family," Chris chuckled. "Can't live with 'em..."

"Can't live without 'em?" Chastity finished.

Chris shrugged. "No. Mostly just can't live with 'em."

She laughed and slid to the side to give him a little shoulder nudge.

Only, there was something serious and, yeah, sad underneath his statement. Chastity's heart strained against her ribs. Sure, she was still as hot and agitated as the dryer she leaned against, but in the last couple of weeks as she'd gotten to know Chris, she'd come to see there was a lot hiding out under his surface. His sizzling, buff, tight-assed surface.

He added liquid detergent to the washer, put the lid loosely back on the jug, then closed the washer's lid. After starting the cycle and setting the jug on top of the lid, he leaned against the washer, crossed his arms, and smiled at her.

"Washing whites has never looked so good." She teased him with a wink.

"Yeah, well, I'm a clean boy. I like things nice and clean."

"Oh yeah?"

"Yep."

"Clean?"

"You bet."

"Everywhere?" She lowered her voice to a sultry purr.

He took the bait, reaching for her. "Almost everywhere." His arms slipped around her waist, tugging her close.

Yep, there was definitely something worth testing out her Johnson jammies on in those jeans.

"Good, because there's a time and place to be dirty."

"Is there?"

She slid her arms up over his shoulders, leaning into him, snuggling her chest against his firm, muscled one. He tilted forward to bring his lips into contact with hers, but unlike the sucking, tonsil-hockey kiss Faith and Cooper had engaged in out there in the living room, Chris's kiss was slow and tender. He nipped and teased, spreading his hands across her back and engaging his full body and hers in the process. Chastity rippled with so much heat that the clothes wouldn't need a commercial dryer before long. Her intended husband-to-be sure did know how to turn a girl to jelly.

When Chris finally eased up enough for both of them to breathe and lowered one hand to cradle her backside, Chastity sighed.

"How come we aren't married yet?" she curled her fingers into the thick curls of Chris's hair.

Chris shrugged, still holding her as close as he could. The splash of the washer filling with water made Chastity think that she might just need to wash her panties if they kept up like this.

"We've still got tons of time before we hit the deadline to marry in Granddaddy's will," he said. "Why rush into anything?"

In spite of the vague twist of frustration that came with his words, Chastity laughed. "I can think of a few reasons to rush." She swiveled her hips into his bulge.

Chris caught his breath and squeezed her backside. "Okay, there's that." He nudged her to the side so that her backside wedged up against the side of the washer, then leaned in for another kiss.

Chastity practically shook as he devoured her. Damn, if he was this good at kissing, how good would he be at everything else? She wanted to rip off his clothes and grab great, big handfuls of muscle and just kiss him all over. *All* over. And she wanted him to do the same to her. In fact, she was sorely tempted to peel off her t-shirt and pop open her bra for him right there, whether they were married or not.

"Besides." Chris stopped kissing her abruptly and went on with their conversation as if she wasn't dripping with need in his arms. "I figure that one of the others will grab this whole situation by the hornies and get pregnant pretty soon. Just like everything else around here, they don't need me to get involved. All they need is my signature on a piece of paper next to yours."

Dammit, that tingly, emotional feeling was back again. She moved her arms to hug him.

"I'm sure your brothers need you for a lot more than a signature." She peeked up at him through her lashes, smiling one of those smiles designed to break through gloom to make him smile too. "I know I need you for more than a signature."

Chris did smile, but it was more of the bittersweet, wistful kind. Not what she'd been going for.

"You know, I like you, Chastity Quinlan," he said.

"You do?" She teased him back.

"Yeah." His grin turned wicked. "I liked you from the first moment you walked into this house."

"Good thing, too, since you're supposed to marry me and all."

"Am I?"

Her mouth dropped open, ready to scold him, but he surprised her into a gasp by lifting her and sitting her on the edge of the washer. In that position, her legs just naturally wanted to spread open. Once she did that, it was only right and proper that Chris should wedge himself and the big old budge in his jeans right into the space where he would do the most good. Chastity's breath came in short gulps as he pressed all the good stuff right into—dammit, why was she wearing clothes at all right then?

"You don't really want to wait until the last minute for vows and rings and…and wedding nights, do you?" Chastity whispered, breathless, as Chris leaned in closer to her.

"Why do we have to wait at all?" His sultry gaze flashed with devilry and desire.

"It's the right thing to do?" Her mama would have been proud. As grating as all those lectures on virginity and saving it for marriage and being pure of body and mind had been, and in spite of a libido that made her dizzy more often than not, Chastity had listened and obeyed.

Of course, that whole being good and obeying thing was next to impossible to do when Chris reached for the fly of her jeans and inched the zipper down, revealing pink, lacy panties.

"You wouldn't dare," she whispered, eyes bright with excitement.

"Wouldn't I?" His voice was deep and scintillating as he teased his fingers along the waist of her jeans, tugging her shirt up so he could spread his hand along the bare skin of her belly.

Chastity jerked and caught her breath and definitely, definitely added to the need for clean underwear. She also bit her lip, hummed deep in her throat, and reached for the zipper of Chris's pants.

She had it halfway down when the washer kicked over from filling to agitating. The sudden jiggling when everything was turned on and amped up was too much—for either of them.

"Oh Lord," Chastity gulped as Chris pressed into her with a growl.

They went from zero to sixty in no time flat. Chris brought his mouth crashing down over hers and his hands sliding up under her t-shirt. Right up under her bra too. Chastity sighed and wriggled her hips against him. The vibration of the washer rubbed the two of them together in excellent ways. Her clothes weren't even off, and she felt like blast-off was imminent. Panting like she'd run a marathon, she reached back to grab hold of something and give herself some leverage—

—and slammed her hand right into the jug of laundry detergent. The jug bumped into the washer controls, then tipped over. The cap went flying off, clattering to the floor. It was a brand new, deluxe-size jug too, and before either of them could blink, silky-blue liquid detergent splashed across the top of the washer. It soaked into the seat of Chastity's already suspiciously damp jeans, leaking down the sides of the washer to the floor, and seeping into the machine itself.

"Are you *that* wet already?" Chris panted, breaking his kiss long enough to peer at Chastity with hooded eyes.

Chastity would have answered, but her hands slipped under the viscous liquid and she jerked backwards. She let out a yelp, but Chris caught her before she could bump her head. That was about all he could do before his arms brushed against the soapy mess on top of the washer.

"What the heck?"

He pulled Chastity toward him to get a look. He also made the mistake of moving his feet...right into the detergent that had spilled to the floor. As he lifted Chastity off the washer, he slid on the slippery floor.

Chastity yelped again as the two of them went down. It was like a slow-motion building collapse...with laundry detergent and suds. No matter what either of them tried to grab onto as they fell, they lost their grip, lost their footing, and ended up in a mountain fresh blob of tangled arms and legs, tinted blue, on the laundry room floor. Half a shelf of dryer sheets, bleach, and other bottles went down with them, along with someone's basket of clean laundry that was waiting to be folded. At least that helped to cushion the fall.

"What just happened?" Chastity panted.

Chris would have answered if the washer hadn't chosen that moment to suds over. Like a giant, bubbly burp, all the liquid soap that had spilled into the load of swishing underwear fizzed over, spilling onto the floor. And there Chris and Chastity were—a twisted tangle of arms and legs, soap and sex, just trying to get up.

Not that kind of up.

"Mom's going to kill me," Chris laughed. He extracted himself from Chastity and looked for a clean spot of linoleum to plant his foot.

"What are they going to think we were doing in here?" Chastity followed suit, looking for some way to stand. It was way harder than she'd ever thought it would be. Soap plus linoleum was the kind of thing that made standing next to impossible, especially with the washing machine continuing to suds over.

"I didn't think laundry detergent was supposed to be that soapy." Chris finally figured out how to brace himself between the dryer and the wall. He reached down to hoist Chastity to her feet.

"I didn't think so either."

Chastity took a second to catch her breath once she was balanced—more or less—in Chris's arms. They were both soaked in fragrant, blue liquid. A piece of her blond hair was matted to the side of her face. Chris's back and butt were plastered with soap, and he had a smudge of blue on the side of his neck.

"God, you look sexy covered in soap," Chastity panted.

"You too."

He dove in for a kiss. Their mouths met and parted, seeking and finding. Unfortunately, they also found the acrid taste of extra-strength detergent, and lost their footing.

They broke apart as they scrambled to stay upright.

"Bleh!" Chastity wiped her mouth with her sleeve. That only got more detergent in her mouth. She starts spitting and grumbling, and somehow managed to make it to the laundry room sink.

Chris was right behind her. Within seconds, they had the tap running and took turns rinsing and spitting out soap.

A knock sounded on the door, followed by Linda asking, "What are you two getting up to in there?"

"She's going to kill me," Chris whispered, staring at the formerly clean, now ruined laundry around them, then called over his shoulder, "Nothing, Mom. Just some spilled soap."

"Spilled soap?" Linda yanked open the door. "Oh my word!"

Soap and suds had begun to leak out under the laundry room door, but Linda's unbelieving gaze settled on Chris and Chastity by the sink, covered in blue goo. At her shout, Karlan and Hope and Faith scrambled out of the living room and into the hall to take a look. Faith burst into laughter at the sight of them, which only caused the others to get up and come running too.

"Chris, you idiot," Cooper laughed as he craned his neck to see the soapy disaster.

"And you wonder why we don't let you mess with anything on the ranch," Kolby added.

"I don't know," Karlan shrugged. "Right now he looks like he could really clean things up."

The three brothers shared a laugh. Chris laughed with him, but from Chastity's way of looking at it, there wasn't much humor in his eyes.

"Come here, Mom, I need a hug," Chris said, starting toward Linda with slippery, outstretched arms.

"Don't you come near me, covered in soap like that," Linda scolded and laughed at the same time. Chris held back, glancing down at the mess of his clothes and the foam on the floor. "I expect you to clean that up," Linda went on.

"Of course, Ma." Chris winked at her, then winced and cried out. "I got soap in my eye."

"Here, I can get it out." Chastity grabbed his hand and pulled him back to the sink.

They spent the next fifteen minutes rinsing themselves off in the sink, then in the shower down the hall, until the only soap left was on the floor and the washer. Then they cleaned that up.

"Well, at least it'll be easy to wash all these towels now that they're filled with soap," Chastity sighed. She rested back on her haunches in a squat on the now squeaky-clean laundry room floor.

"I guess so." Chris tossed he towel he'd been using onto the pile the two of them had made, then flopped to sit against the wall. "So what are we going to do?" he asked, sounding a little too defeated for Chastity's liking.

Chastity shrugged. "Sex in the laundry room is out, *that* much is for sure."

Chris chuckled. "We could try it in the kitchen."

Chastity wrinkled her nose. "Too unhygienic. People eat in there."

"How about the stable?"

"Nah, the horses would give us funny looks. Plus, hay."

Chris chuckled. "The car then?"

"Too cramped."

"I give up."

Chastity grinned. This was fun. No one had ever really bantered with her before. Argued, yes. She was forever arguing and bickering with her sisters and her parents. But nothing had ever come close to this silly back and forth about ridiculous things. Yeah, she knew she was weird and different, but Chris didn't seem to mind at all. In fact, he was smiling at her now like he wanted to go through the whole soap-up again.

"Well," she sighed. "There really isn't anything else we can do."

"We could always get married." Chris shrugged.

"You think?" She pretended as though no one had ever thought of the idea before.

"Why not?" Chris grinned. "At least then we'd have the full green-light to go ahead and get our nasty on in an actual bed."

"What, and miss out on all the soap?"

"We could bring a bottle of scented hand soap into bed with us."

Chastity pretended to consider, tilting her head to the side. "Doesn't that stuff have a lot of alcohol in it? It could sting really bad in...places."

Chris laughed. "I hadn't thought of that." He rolled to his knees and crawled across the laundry room floor to her. "We'll just have to buy a really big bottle of lube instead and slick ourselves down."

It was Chastity's turn to laugh, but that laughter was cut short as Chris moved in for a kiss. One of the good kisses—not too hard, not too soft. Just right. It left her head spinning and her heart—and other regions—on fire.

"Let's get married," he whispered, rocking back to grin at her. "Just you and me, at the church tomorrow. No one else invited."

She never would have guessed that the idea of getting married without her sisters would be so appealing, but at that moment, all she wanted was Chris, now and forever.

"Okay," she said with a fake casual shrug. "I've got nothing better to do tomorrow."

Chris stole another quick kiss, winked at her, then stood, pulling her up with him. "All right then. It's a date. You and me and Brother Anthony. And then we'll finish what we started here. Without soap."

www.ingramcontent.com/pod-product-compliance
Lightning Source LLC
Chambersburg PA
CBHW031336160726
47993CB00002B/701